BEAUTIFUL MONSTER

Also By Bella Forrest:

A Shade Of Vampire

A Shade Of Blood

www.bellaforrest.net

NASHVILLE PUBLIC LIBRARY
FOUNDATION

*This book
made possible
through generous gifts
to the
Nashville Public Library
Foundation Book Fund*

NPLF.ORG

ALL RIGHTS RESERVED BY AUTHOR

Published by Bella Forrest

Copyright © 2013 by Bella Forrest.

TABLE OF CONTENTS

PROLOGUE - AMY

I always used to picture myself in some sort of fairy tale. I had my life all planned out. I would be a famous actress and everyone would tell me my talent was beyond words. I would be able to bring tears of joy or happiness to any audience's eyes in seconds, and be able to portray even the hardest of characters in the blink of an eye. If I were really famous, and there were tabloids written about me, they would say I was beautiful (somehow, my hair color was always a perfect blond and I was tall and graceful). And I would have a perfect husband by my side; who supported me, loved every part of me, and was just as beautiful. He would always be fun to be around, and we would never argue. The world would adore him too; but they would respect our love.

And, in these dreams, I wasn't sick. I never was. There were no endless needles or pills; no concerned looks and long hours in the doctor's office. My purse wasn't filled with medication; I was always full of energy, I didn't have "bad days." I was the picture of health and nothing could hold me back.

Falling in love with Liam hadn't been exactly what I pictured; but when I look back, I wouldn't have it any other way. All those men whom I imagined as my perfect love don't compare to him.

Liam isn't perfect, of course, but somehow, I love him in ways I never thought possible. His pain, his past, who he is, everything that would be considered an "imperfection" are just reasons why I love him more. What we have been through in this short period is more than any couple has been able to withstand in a thousand lifetimes.

He is always there for me; always supports and protects me; always finds a way to make me feel safe, even in the darkness. At first, when we met, I thought he was distant, emotionless, and

1

there wasn't a thing in the world that could make me give him a second thought. But time heals all wounds and changes thoughts. And of course, here we are now.

I don't know what the future holds for Liam and me. My mortality looms every day, and every second I draw breath is one step closer to being six feet under. But I do know, as long as I draw breath I will be by his side.

<u>PREFACE - LIAM</u>

I had known something was different about her from the moment she walked onto the stage, looking like a startled deer. Had it been any other auditionee—and there were hundreds who showed up looking afraid—I would have immediately drawn an "x" through their name and written them off without a second thought. But she was different, and not just because she was good. She was better than good. When she spoke, the words came out as if they were natural—something I continuously tried to beat into students' heads without much success.

And she was beautiful, but that was inconsequential. Most actresses are some type of beauty, or they make you believe so. And this is a tough industry. It's not seen through rose-tinted glasses. If I can't see some sort of physical beauty in them, even at this young age, then they don't get a shot. Better they learn it here than somewhere else.

Speaking of shots, I had certainly had at least two too many last night. It was a rough night - rougher than most. It seems closer to a full moon, the cravings always get worse. I'm not sure why, and I haven't bothered to figure it out, but come the full moon, the urge to feed on human blood is never stronger. The alcohol helps, although it isn't always a cure.

Which led to that morning, and my pounding head. Curse immortality that comes with hangovers. I still suffer the effects nearly every time. And when walking into a room full of energized, over-dramatic teenagers, the symptoms double.

I nodded curtly to a few of them and made my way toward the front of the room. Some of them called my name—no doubt they had questions about the latest simple assignment I'd given them. No matter how simple I made the homework, they had questions.

3

I was leaning against my desk with my back to them to try to drown out the noise, when suddenly the pain started to subside. The room was growing quiet, and the scent of human blood was neutralized.

I took a deep, pain free breath and turned around, proud of myself for controlling the urge. But then I saw I had not done so at all.

She was standing in the center of the now quiet room, blushing at the curious stares. Her long hair was hanging straight down her back, her huge brown eyes that had first attracted me were staring right into my own. But it was her scent; calming my urges, that made me hold her gaze as I wondered what she was. I felt better almost instantly, swallowing to find the words to speak.

"Take a seat, Amy." I said, gesturing with my free hand, and she nodded, sitting down almost instantly. "And the rest of you..." I said, giving them my usual glare. They scuttled to their seats, pulling out notebooks. I couldn't keep my eyes off her the entire lesson. What was she? What was drawing me to her? What story of us was just beginning?

CHAPTER 1: AMY

Write about what you want to be when you grow up. What made you decide that? Use all the proper formatting described in the previous chapter. I read the assignment over and over again before I clicked the start button. The thing with being homeschooled, or 'online schooled,' was that once I clicked the start button for the test, I couldn't do things normal students did, like negotiate for extra time to go to the bathroom, or argue my grade. I had to do it right the first time.

I glanced at the clock, seeing that I still had about forty five minutes left before Dad came home. The assignment was only allotted at thirty minutes, maximum, which meant I could probably finish it in twenty. They always gave you too much time with these things, which was silly really, because it meant you had extra time to use the textbook and cheat.

I never cheated, of course. I just couldn't bring myself to do it. My father had taught me that something worth doing was worth doing right, and even if he wasn't home, his lessons rung loud in my ears. If I started this assignment right away, I could finish it and start dinner. I was planning stuffed peppers worthy of a five star restaurant—my father would expect no less—and when I read the recipe for them, I almost drooled. However, they would take some time to make, and I didn't want him home and waiting on food, not after a long day at work.

I clicked start, taking a deep breath, and positioned my fingers over the keyboard. *Go.*

I want to be an actress. I think I've always wanted to be an actress. I can remember, when I was young, putting on plays for my parents and my stuffed animals in the living room. Nothing thrilled me more than dressing up in costumes, making up stories and performing at the top of my lungs. However, I think there was one day when it became more than just a childhood fantasy.

I was nine years old, and my father and I had just moved here. After months of job searching, he finally got a job at a prestigious theater school just down the road. He was to be a cook, helping with not just the students' three meals a day and snacks (about 50% of the students are boarders), but also the catering for the fancy theatrical events and any food props needed for the shows. It meant long hours, but that made up for the low pay. I remember him working late at home one night trying to develop a way for meat to be raw on the outside, but cooked on the inside. Whatever show they were doing at the time was not 'appropriate for a child of my age,' but he succeeded, and they put his name in the program and gave him 'special thanks' along with the rest of the chefs.

One day, he asked me if I would like to come to work with him. It was national 'take your child to work day,' and workplaces all across the country were participating. It sounded much better than being at my tutor's place all day (in those days, I was tutored; it was just a few years before we discovered I could get a good education online), so I agreed. I was surprised that he would let me out of the house for so long. You see, the other thing you should know about me, is that before this, I hadn't dared to really have dreams. My mother died of AIDS when I was just a baby, and while my father was lucky enough to escape being infected, her blood runs through my veins. I was diagnosed as HIV positive when I was barely a week old.

My father has always been overly protective of me, keeping me homeschooled, warning me not to exert myself, barely letting me be in contact with other people. And while I understand his concern, things are different now than in my mother's time. People with HIV can survive for years living a normal life, and even once the virus becomes full blown AIDS, ten or twenty years are not unheard of. I try not to think about when that will happen, because it's inevitable. For now, I have mostly good days. Lonely, but good days.

Anyway, I'm getting off-topic. The point is, the next day I was up at the crack of dawn, dressed in my best clothes, making my hair as neat as possible, excited to go to work with him. We left earlier than he normally would so that we could walk together. I was practically bouncing off the walls.

The school was the most beautiful thing I had ever seen: historic and sturdy on the outside, and the walls inside were filled with colors. There were murals, art work and old photographs from shows mounted on the walls. There were hundreds of black and white pictures of the students in various plays, their costumes and makeup outstanding. I had never seen anything so beautiful in all my life. But that wasn't the best part.

Dad had me sit on a stool with him, watching him take orders and cook up breakfast for the two hundred students about to arrive at the cafeteria. But when breakfast was over, he winked at me and told me this was the best part of the job; that he could take long breaks in between. He led me down the hallway to the grand theater which was placed in the center of the school. Putting a finger to his lips to signal that I should be quiet, he opened the door and snuck me into the back row. On stage, the lights dimmed and the soundtrack played. Rehearsals for that year's production were just starting.

This is when my fate was decided. I don't think I closed my mouth the entire time we were there. I didn't say a word; my mouth just hung open in awe. That year they were doing a musical—Les Miserables—and their opening night was just days away. The actors were ready to perform, with their lines memorized and dance steps learned. I watched, as if I were in a dream, as they entered the stage, one by one, their costumes grand and elaborate, and their performances spot on. I cried when Fantine perished, and clapped when Cossette was safe. I sat on the edge of my seat, my hands over my eyes, as Javert ran about the stage, looking for his prey. And when it was over, my eyes were sparkling. I was on my feet, applauding and cheering.

"Did you like that?" Dad asked, beside me, reaching out to stroke my hair. And then I turned to him, and sealed my fate.

"Dad, I want to be an actress."

It was out of the question, before the words even left my mouth. He was too protective of me. I was too fragile. The tuition fees were too high, even if I stayed at home and became only a day

7

student. They had a rigorous audition process, and students from around the world came to try out—having been trained and performing since they could walk. Students who were to grace the stages of this school would go on to appear in Hollywood; their names in lights. They would sing on Broadway and at the Metropolitan Opera. They would tour the world. Their parents were wealthy - perhaps successful actors themselves. This was not the school for a chef's daughter who had a dream, and nothing more.

That was nine years ago, and I haven't forgotten a moment of that day. Although it may not be a reality, this essay asked what I wanted to be when I grew up, not what I was going to be. Every year, I watch the Oscars with the knowledge of one who has seen the films a thousand times. I download bootleg copies of West End performances, and order theater textbooks from university bookstores, even though I'm not enrolled in their courses. I think every single one of my pleasure reads is about actors, about the stage or the screen. I still memorize monologues and I post them on YouTube, although no one ever watches. It doesn't matter. The pure joy of doing that is enough for me.

My father thinks that this was the last I knew of the school. Sure, we go to see the shows, and I occasionally talk to him about the actors we've seen there. But to the best of his knowledge, I spend the rest of my time at home, working hard to get high grades to go to a good college. He wants me to be a writer, or a researcher—perhaps a historian—with a Master's degree or a PhD. He wants better for me than what he has—only an 8th grade education and minimum wage to support us. He hasn't taken me to work since that day when I was nine; it's as if, even then, I was outgrowing his profession, I was better than that. He wants me to find something unstressful that has flexible hours that I can do from home. But home is the last place I want to be.

At least twice a week, I wait until I know he's busy in the kitchens, and I sneak into the school. I could navigate the route in my sleep by now. The classrooms are mini theaters in and of themselves, and there are so many observers and auditors - local drama classes coming for field trips and potential students - that no one notices if I sneak in. I always sit at the back, knowing where to *hide out of the light. I could sit for days on end listening to the lectures and watching the rehearsals. By the time we go to see the shows, I know every line and step off by heart. I can sing every note, bring every emotion forward, and recite every line. I try to follow along with my age group, so I never look too suspicious sitting in the back row. The lectures and lessons are different from year to year, and I always take notes. I have notebooks full of them, hidden under my bed upstairs. Although sometimes, it's a pleasure to watch the first year students, just six or seven years old, acting out performances well beyond their years, without even breaking a sweat. I know the theories of Stanislavski and Uta Hagen like the back of my hand. I know stage right, stage left, upstage, downstage, backstage, everything. I can listen to almost any Shakespeare quote and tell you who said it, where it's from, and what it means.*

Most of the students, they don't stay the full twelve years there. They enter late, or leave early, either for fame and fortune, or because of broken dreams. Some of them barely make it a year, the classes are anything but easy, and the directors are as hard on them as they would be to any professional actor. I probably have been there longer than any of them, with nine years of sneaking in under my belt. I long to be in front of an audience of more than my stuffed animals and five people on YouTube, to try to apply what I've learned.

But I've learned to face reality. I've not been able to go to the school for a week or so at a time when I've been ill myself, and I realize how lucky I have it. When my energy is low, I just have to open my laptop. But when I finally do make it back, I feel so full of life. The school rejuvenates me.

So that's what I want to be when I grow up, an actress. And that was the day I decided it forever.

I hit save, and spell check, re-reading quickly before I hit submit and ended the test. I wanted to forget writing it as soon as I was done; bringing back up those feelings was going to stick with me. As soon as I saw it was submitted, I shut down the computer and got up to stretch. I had been typing for four straight hours, finishing most of my assignments, ahead of time as usual. But now, Dad would be home, and I wanted to get a head start on dinner.

Most of my ingredients had already been prepared in the professional way that he had taught me. I had learned about food safety before I learned not to stick my fingers in light sockets. I couldn't help putting some in my mouth as I was preparing it, everything tasted so good today. Some days, my appetite seemed to leave me, but at that moment it had returned with a vengeance.

Just 62 days until Oscar Nominations posted! My phone beeped with a text from my friend, Sarah. Sarah was my kindred spirit, my best friend. We had met online via a forum where we were discussing actors and movies, and we exchanged phone numbers the next day. Despite having never met, we texted each other several times a day with little updates and messages.

I smiled, typing back a huge smiley face, and then went back to stuffing peppers. Dad had warned me that this was my one downfall in the kitchen; my phone. I teased him that one day, I would make fried cell phone, and his face showed that he wouldn't put it past me.

Is your Dad home yet? Does he know who is cast in this year's winter performance? That beautiful HBO–pretty Luke you wrote me about?

I glanced at the clock before replying. Although I couldn't attend the school, I badgered Dad for information, and always saw every performance they put on. This year, the most promising of all was a senior named Luke, who had the lead in every show. The last show's program said he already had an agent and would be moving to LA as soon as his schooling was done.

Not home yet, but soon. I'll tell you as soon as I know, but I don't know when they are posting the cast list.

Living next door to a theater school was like having my own personal Hollywood, and at least I had Sarah to share it with, rather than sitting in silence all day long.

10

The clock chimed 6pm just as I heard the door open. Dad was a bit late, but not overly so.

"Hi!" I called to him, turning around just as I finished the last of the cutting. He smiled at me as he stepped into the kitchen.

"There are only two professions in the world where one is used to being greeted with a huge knife. Serial Killer and Chef. Be careful, Amy."

"Sorry," I said, turning around and putting it down again before giving him a hug. Being homeschooled often meant I didn't see another living soul all day. "You're late. Was the cast list posted for the winter show?"

"What?" He looked at me, confused, before he clicked in. "Oh. I don't know."

"You don't know?" I gave him a horrified look. How exactly could he spend all day there and not know? "But it was due any day now. And isn't that why you were late? Students all checking the cast list?"

"The headmaster was going on and on about the use of so much red meat in food," he replied, hanging up his coat. "These may be drama students, rising stars, but they are still normal kids who like burgers and fries. Geez... Anyway, what are you cooking?"

"Stuffed Peppers." I had begun to set the table, wondering exactly how messy these peppers were going to be.

"Did you finish your assignments today, or do you need to continue to work?" he asked, and I nodded.

"No, I'm done. I'm so glad I don't have to take calculus any longer." Calculus had been the bane of my existence, and it was mandatory up until 10th grade. I wasn't sure exactly what I was going to do with my life, but I knew math wasn't going to be in it, so the moment it became optional, I had stopped. When I had math on my plate in 8th and 9th grade, and had begun taking courses online by myself, I had spent about every evening in tears trying to figure it

11

out. Dad had not been much help then, having stopped taking math in 8th grade himself, to train as an apprentice chef. It hadn't helped that he had told me, with a rueful smile, that math was also the bane of my mother's existence when she was in school. I just felt more doomed than ever before.

"What did you do today, then?" he asked, reaching to pour himself a glass of water.

"English, mostly," I replied. "A little French and world politics." I took a breath before posing my next question. However, before I could ask him about colleges, he cut me off.

"And how are you feeling?"

"Fine," I replied, a bit annoyed. This was his question almost every minute of the day. I received two phone calls and five text messages a day from him, asking the same thing. "I even cleaned my room during lunch."

"Are you sure you're feeling fine, then? You cleaned your room?" He gave me a teasing glance. "Who are you and what have you done with my daughter?"

"Aliens," I replied, as the oven dinged. "That's what happens when you get left alone all day. You're an easy target for abduction." I pulled the food out of the oven, putting it on hot plates on the table.

"Tomorrow I'll be late again," Dad said, as he sat down, taking another swallow of water. "Possibly into the evening. In fact, it'll likely be that way all next week."

"Oh?" I looked up, surprised. Tomorrow was Friday, and we usually rented a film and ordered in dinner. It had been a tradition since my childhood, and while the movies had changed from cartoons to dramas, the ritual remained the same.

"Next week they are having auditions for the winter semester, so they'll have an overload of potential students flooding the school, which means the cafeteria will be extra busy. I need to make sure things are prepped and ready so we don't get slammed. The last thing the headmaster will want is for us to appear as though we are not top quality. Even if that means we've just run out of fries and pizza."

"Anyone interesting?"

"Just mostly potential transfers from that drama school down south," he replied, chewing thoughtfully. "You practically have to have a pedigree to get into a school full of pedigrees."

"Right," I replied, taking a bite. "How is it?" I asked, alarmed, when he put his fork down after only one bite.

"It's fine. Good herbs, not bad on the sauce. It's just..." After a minute he pushed his plate away. "Sorry, Amy, I'm just not very hungry today. My stomach has been upset since breakfast."

"Oh!" I replied, but he shook his head and gave me a soft smile. "Nothing to worry about, love. It really is good."

"Good enough for a professional chef?" I asked, and his face darkened.

"You need to set your sights higher than that, Amy. Speaking of, when are college applications due?"

"Next month." I replied. "But I looked into it today. I mean...you don't just fill out a form and submit as many as you like. They cost money to even submit. It's about 100, each time."

He winced at this, meeting my eyes.

"100? For each one?"

"More for the private schools," I said, looking down. "And that's for online applications too. But Dad, we don't have to..." The last thing I wanted to be was a burden. Already, I had seen my father go without a hat or warm coat because of the cost of my medication.

"Don't be silly. This is your future," he said, standing up and carrying his plate to the sink. "We'll figure it out, one way or another, and I don't want to hear another word about it. Submit as many as you can, Amy."

"But..." I started, and he glared at me.

"The discussion is closed." He rinsed his plate, his back to me. "Now I'm going to lie down for a bit, see if I can't shake this. I'll do the dishes later tonight. You should get a head start on those applications, look into them and see how many you'd like to submit."

"All right," I replied, reluctantly. I already knew in my head that the number was in the double digits, if I could have my way, and I knew that there was no way we could pay for it. But Dad wasn't giving me a chance to protest, and before I could say another word, he was gone.

After I finished my own dinner, I rebooted my computer and brought my notebook to the kitchen table. Turning to a blank page and trying to ignore the pages already filled with theater notes, I wrote *College*, in big letters on the top of a page, and began to write down admission requirements for each. However, each time I clicked on a page full of the list of programs, I couldn't help but check out the requirements for the Theater Majors. Most required an audition, although I knew already which were good schools and which were not. College or not, none of them compared to the education offered at the theater school down the road, but perhaps it could be another dream of mine.

I was interrupted by the sound of footsteps upstairs, and then, to my horror, my father choking. I shut my notebook in a hurry, heading to the bottom of the stairs. "Dad?" I called, and after a long silence, he responded.

"I'm alright, Amy. Just an upset stomach."

"Oh no." I came a few steps up to the landing, where I could see him leaning over the sink. He looked terrible, the transformation from just an hour ago was stunning. Pale and

14

sweaty, his jaw clenched as tightly as his hands, he looked like he was about to fall over. "Are you sure you're alright?"

"No, stay away." He waved an arm at me.

"You think you have a bug or something?"

"Chef's curse," he said, with a shaky grin. "I've felt it before. I think the milk from this morning might have gone bad."

"You don't think it was my peppers, do you?" I asked, alarmed that I might have done something careless.

"No." He shook his head. "If it was, you'd be sick, but it also wouldn't have come on so fast. We had leftovers among the kitchen staff this morning which tasted off. I ignored it then, but that's probably what it is now. Still, if it's contagious, I don't want you too close, Amy. I want you to stay downstairs, and wash your hands."

"Can I get you anything?" I offered, unsure of what to do. My father was my rock, my stronghold, and seeing him weakened was frightening to me.

"No, thank you, darling. Just stay downstairs. I'm sure I'll be fine in the morning."

"Right," I said, not believing that he could go from looking so wretched to making a fast recovery. Still, I listened to his wishes, and backtracked down the stairs.

Parts haven't been cast yet, and I think I food poisoned my father. I failed you on both fronts. I texted Sarah once I was back in the kitchen.

I've got something that will cheer you up. She replied, sending me a link. With a smile, I clicked on it, and sat back in my chair watching Dame Judy Dench perform Shakespeare at London's West End. Sarah always knew how to save the day. Thank God for best friends, even ones so far away.

CHAPTER 2: AMY

I opened my eyes to a now familiar sound—that of my father coughing in the early morning light. This had been going on for a week and it wasn't getting any better. What he thought was just food poisoning was either the worst case that had ever existed, or something more. Either way, I was suffering along with him. Not just from seeing him in pain, but from his lack of work. The chefs relied not only on their salaries, but also on tips that were shared with the staff when they catered big events. Dad had not been to work for a week. When I checked the bank account online yesterday, which should have been payday, I was shocked to find a negative amount. And it was two more weeks until he got paid again. We needed money; we were already only just getting by. We couldn't go on like this.

"Dad," I said, appearing in his room as the sun rose. I was dressed in black pants and a white shirt with my jacket on. The moment he saw me, I'm sure he knew what I was going to do.

"Amy, no."

"And why not, exactly?" I asked, leaning against the doorpost. "Have you seen the amount of money we have lately?"

"Amy." He sat up, trying to take a sip of water, but finding his stomach wouldn't have any of it. "This isn't what I wanted for you, to ever have to do this."

"Don't be dramatic, Dad," I said. "Leave that for the students. It's not forever. It's just for a few days, until you feel better."

"You're better than this," he managed, and I sighed.

"If it's good enough for you forever, it's good enough for me. It'll be fine, Daddy, don't worry. It was fine when I spent those few weeks working with you a summer ago."

"That was…" He gasped at the pain in his stomach, wincing for a moment, and then continued. "That was for work experience, for your college applications. You shouldn't have to worry about money or jobs, or any of this."

"Well, maybe I need more work experience. Other girls my age have much more experience than me, at multiple jobs. A few more days can only inch closer to looking good," I said, with a half-smile. I knew him too well. We would argue for another few minutes, and then he would let me have my way. That's how it always was.

"How are you feeling?" he asked and I raised my eyebrow, finding it funny that in light of the situation, he was the one asking me this.

"I feel fine, I swear," I replied. "And my cell phone is fully charged, I promise I'll call you every break."

Eventually, he sighed, too tired to argue. And he knew I was speaking sense; he had seen the contents of the fridge. I was doing what was necessary.

"All right," he said, finally. "Call me every break. And I know when they are."

"Of course," I replied, blowing him a kiss from the doorway. "Can I bring you anything else?"

"You'll be late," he said to me, and I grinned, nodding as I closed the door behind me. As soon as I was outside, in the early morning sunshine, I texted Sarah.

He said yes! To the school I go.

The reply came back almost instantly.

TELL ME EVERYTHING! Oh my God, SO LUCKY!

I smiled at this. When Sarah and I had discussed it last night, I thought it would be impossible. But now as I walked toward the school, it felt like I was living a dream.

Even if I had not spent every second day sneaking around the school, I had spent enough time there legally to know it like the back of my hand. There were no first day jitters, no fears of the unfamiliar that usually accompanied entering a new place. Instead, I was full of energy with a huge smile on my face when I slid through the back door of the kitchen.

"Watch out, Trouble Jr. is here!" called out Adam, who was my Dad's right-hand man, and had known me since I was a child. I grinned, opening my mouth to explain the situation, but Adam shook his head. "He already spoke to me, kid. You're not the only one who can communicate with a cell phone."

I laughed at that, slipping my phone into my back pocket. "So, what's happening today?"

"Big group of people today, few different events going on," Adam said, as he led me toward the back so I could get an apron and cap. "Now, listen, Amy, I know it's hard to cook with gloves, but..."

"You need me to, in case I cut my hand off and blood goes everywhere," I replied, with a tight smile. "I know. Don't worry about it"

"Don't cut your hand off, your father will be mad," Adam replied, trying to lighten the situation. "That's a general rule for all chefs."

"Right." I nodded, and shooed him out so I could suit up. Feeling a bit like I was a surgeon preparing for an operation, I exited the changing room and headed for the prep line.

"All right, can you cut up these veggies?" Adam asked. I nodded. "We need enough for an army, so don't stop until you can't find another vegetable in this kitchen. You get three coffee breaks and an hour for lunch, but I'll let you take them whenever you need, kid. Just pace yourself and be..."

"Careful," I finished the sentence with an eye roll, and then rolled up my sleeves in order to wash the massive pile of vegetables in the tin bowl in front of me. The vegetables were meant to go with a homemade dip that was being prepared opposite me. Nothing at this school was done simply. I knew that simple cubes of cucumber or carrot sticks weren't going to suffice. Instead, I cut shapes, stars, circles and squares, making a rainbow array of colors and shapes, arranging them on platter after platter. I smiled as I worked, listening to the conversations around me. It was so nice to be out of the house and around people. Still, my heart hammered every time I looked at the clock. I was timing my three breaks so that each one would coincide with catching a bit of my favorite classes, or seeing my favorite instructors. If I could slip in just three times today, it would be enough to keep me happy for another few days.

It was like an addiction, seeing the classes run, watching the rehearsals. I had read the symptoms of addiction for a course last year and it all fit—dependency, need to lie, first thing you think about when you wake up, etc. But it could be worse. *I could be doing drugs. Illegal ones,* I thought to myself with a little laugh as I cut up a red pepper into the shape of a star. Legal ones, I'd been doing since birth. HIV positive patients had enough drugs prescribed to them to run a small pharmacy.

When the clock struck 10:15, I stopped and headed to the back to take off my apron, gloves and hairnet. "Going for coffee!" I called to Adam, who nodded at me, absorbed in his work. I could probably go to the moon and he wouldn't have noticed, as long as I got the vegetables done.

Pulling my hair into a bun and trying to repair the damage the hairnet had caused, I zipped up my jacket so as to not look so obviously like a chef. The students around me wore an array of colors, except for the senior ones who were currently in rehearsal week for physical theater. They were required to wear all black, all the time, and you could always spot them in the crowd.

I was heading toward room 3C, a huge lecture hall, in order to catch a lecture on Kabuki theater, when I was distracted by a girl's bright yellow poodle skirt. Suddenly I felt my body connect with someone else's. The force of it made me stumble back a little and I narrowly missed the lockers.

I knew instantly whom I'd walked into. It wasn't hard to recognize him after all these years. Always surrounded by a cloud of staff, as if he was too good to even brush elbows with the students, stood Liam Swift. He glanced back at me quickly as he continued walking, and our eyes met, just once, before his entourage continued to sweep him away.

Liam Swift. Sarah and I practically had a heart attack when he rose to Hollywood fame. He was insanely gorgeous, probably one of the best looking men I had ever seen, with piercing light grey eyes, and dark, almost black hair kept a little too long, so that soft strands were almost touching his eyes. With pale skin, and a lean, muscular body, he was enough to make any girl fall over and do his bidding. Still, despite being stunning, he was one of many Hollywood actors we obsessed over.

At the peak of his career, Sarah had unearthed the fact that his grandfather, Peter, ran a theater school—this school. This discovery alone was enough to draw me here more often than usual. But three years ago, in a flurry of media announcements that had me glued to the local news, Liam had come to our town.

Hollywood Superstar Liam Swift , just twenty-three years old and already on Forbes rich list, announces that he will be taking over the role of headmaster at Leopard Academy, a prestigious theater school founded by his grandfather, Peter Smith. Liam will begin his new duties in September of this year, officially retiring from filmmaking.

I could still hear the newscaster's voice in my ears as she made that announcement. My heart was pounding and I could hardly believe it.

The media had gone crazy, covering every event, attempting to get a glimpse of their favorite star. But now, it had pretty much died down, letting the school function as normal. In fact, the only one who seemed not to function as normal was this egotistic stuck-up headmaster, who never said a kind word to anyone. He always traveled with an entourage of other teachers and I hadn't ever seen a student approach him.

His classes were small and protected, as they were mostly the junior and senior ones, so I had never attended any of them. But while I was curious about his technique, I could study it by watching his movies a million times. His personality, up close, didn't seem worth chasing after. But those eyes ... perhaps those eyes would change my mind.

I shook myself out of my own thoughts, opening the door to the lecture hall and going to sit in the back row. No one noticed. As usual, the class was full of energy and excitement, even though it was just a lecture.

For the next ten minutes, I floated on the professors words, watching image after image of Kabuki style theater float by on the big screen, listening to the techniques each type of actor would apply.

I didn't have my notebook with me, but I took notes on my phone, until it buzzed, reminding me to get back to the kitchen. With a sigh, I waited until the professor changed slides and then slipped out, hurrying back to the vegetables.

"Amy, call your father," Adam said, the second I slipped back in. I reached to pull out my phone and dialed home, while trying to pull my hair net back on with the other hand.

"Amy?" Dad asked, the moment he picked up.

"Yes, I'm fine. Just had first break," I said, as I tied the apron with difficulty. "I'm cutting vegetables all day, nothing I can't handle."

"Good. I told Adam to give you something easy. How are you feeling?"

"I just told you, I'm fine. How are *you* feeling?" I countered, glancing at my appearance in the mirror. *Glamorous*, I thought, sarcastically.

"Better. You shouldn't have to be there much longer, Amy."

"Take as long as you need, Dad," I replied, leaning on the phone so I could straighten my apron. "Really. I'm ahead on school work, so it's not a big deal."

"Just be careful," he told me again, and then bid me goodbye. However, not before making me promise to call him on my next break. I did, and hung up, putting the phone into my purse. If he was going to ring me several times, at least it would be back here.

"Do you want to make a prop?" Adam asked me, approaching with two grocery bags. I nodded, anything was better than cutting vegetables. Peeking inside, I found exactly what I was hoping for.

"We're making fake blood!"

Adam laughed at my delight. "Yes. There's an accident scene in one of the freshman classes, so they need a lot of fake blood. But you've gotta play with it a bit. It's got to look real, but thinner, be easily wiped off, because in the next scene, they are fine."

"Right." I nodded, my mind already turning. Fake blood was easy: corn syrup, food coloring and water. I was already thinking that making it with ice-cubes instead of hot water would keep it thinner and easier to wipe off, without losing its realism.

I set right to work, mixing, stirring and testing. I could only imagine the scenarios in my head for what they would need it for; the creativity that required playing injured. Perhaps the actor would have to fake cry? That was my favorite thing to learn how to do: I had practiced in front of my bedroom mirrors for weeks before I learned how to make tears come on cue. I had been so excited that I almost cried for real. *Of course*, I thought sadly as I stirred a bubbling potful of fake blood, *that was for fun. They need this for real. Lucky.*

I had become so lost in my own thoughts that I barely noticed the hours slip by. But when my stomach grumbled, I was

23

surprised to look up at the clock and find it was 12:50pm. *Perfect,* I thought. I had brought a sandwich and could eat it in the back of the theater. They were rehearsing act one of their production in there this afternoon, and I couldn't wait to watch it with full lighting.

"LUNCH!" I called to Adam. "Oh, and I think the blood's ready. Worthy of any vampire." I grinned, pulling the spoon out to show him the consistency. He raised an eyebrow, coming over to test it on the inside of his wrist.

"Hey, that's not bad," he replied, nodding. "You want me to send this over?"

"Sure, just let it cool, but I think it's done." I replied, pulling off my apron and wiping my hands on it. It certainly looked like blood, even as it dried, darker than when it was wet. "See you after lunch."

"Call your father!" he called after me, and I turned, giving him a thumbs up, before heading into the change room.

I texted Dad this time, quickly, as I hurried down the halls. I didn't want to miss the start of the show, and my sandwich was finished before I had even entered the next building.

On lunch. Going to read a book. I wrote. It was a lame excuse, but he would believe it. I always had my nose in a book, what else was there to do at home? I put my phone away, rounding the corner, attempting to slip into the hall quietly. I did not expect what I was met with.

There were loud voices coming from the hallway. It was impossible to make out individual words in the din. There were at least a hundred girls, maybe more, in a queue that snaked around the hallway and into the next one.

I stopped short before I almost ran into somebody. This had happened before, when I was trying to watch a show. They sometimes invited neighboring schools to watch dress rehearsals, various young drama classes and such. These girls must be from the girls' school on the south side of town. All of them were perfect; tall, thin and beautiful; the type that a private school usually attracts. I immediately felt inadequate, with my thrift store clothes, and hair a mess, not wearing a scrap of makeup.

Self-consciously, I attempted to pull my hair back into a bun, and prayed it would stay that way. I moved past the girls, who were standing in single file. I figured if they were all from one school, they had to stay together, and I could slip past them and get a good seat before they were all gone.

There was a commotion up front and I knew who it was before I even looked up. *Liam.* Escorted as usual by his entourage, I was surprised to also find a crowd of media. That hadn't happened here in a while and I assumed they had given up on him. But here they were, squawking, cameras flashing, as if he hadn't ever been away from Hollywood at all.

One of his entourage had her hand on his back, a tall wiry redhead who looked young enough to be a student herself, pushing him gently through the crowd. Liam was holding a newspaper up to his face, shielding his face from view. However, standing on the other side, I could see he looked tense, paler than this morning, his jaw tightly clenched. And then he was gone, inside the auditorium, and I found myself standing outside the doors.

"Right this way," someone said, and I looked up. She was a 6th grade student, I recognized her from the hallways, and the few times I sat in during her classes. She was shoving a paper into my hand, and hurrying me inside. "Move along please. Only students, no one else."

"What?" I asked my heart in my chest. Did she know my secret? After all these years, was it going to be a preteen girl who called me out? But she seemed already to be speaking to someone else, a mother standing at the front of the line with her arms around someone who was obviously her daughter. I ducked into the room before anyone else had spotted me, heading to the second row to take a seat. Only then did I look down at what was in my hand.

Auditions—Leopard Academy Scholarship Fund—Girls' Day.

Below it was a script; an excerpt from what I quickly read was Beauty and the Beast. But it was the headline that got me. I must have gotten my dates mixed up—today was not the dress rehearsal. Today was the auditions for the scholarship that everyone always buzzed about. Every two years, Leopard Academy held auditions for one talented student to win a full scholarship to the school, for as long as they needed to attend before graduating. This was an old tradition that Liam's grandfather had started, although I imagine it was even more popular now that Liam was the headmaster. The spots were coveted; people came from other countries just to be here today. And here I was, sitting in the second row, technically in line.

Before I could even get to my feet, or pull out my phone to text Sarah, another girl sat beside me, putting her feet up on the chair in front of us.

"Hi. I'm Alicia."

"Uh ... Amy," I said, reaching out to shake hands.

"Did you bring a hardcopy of your headshot and résumé?" Alicia asked, rummaging through her bag frantically. "I mean, of course, I sent it online, but I wasn't sure if we were supposed to bring a hard copy too?"

"Uh ... no," I replied, with a shrug. After all, it was the truth, I wasn't carrying a hardcopy of my headshot and resume with me. Never mind that I didn't actually have either.

"Oh. Well, I'm sure it's fine then." She settled back into her seat, relaxing. "How long have you been acting?"

"Uh…not long," I managed, looking at my watch. This place was packed and it was starting to look like even if I wanted to leave, I couldn't. Not without attracting a lot of attention to myself. "You?"

"Since I was a fetus," she replied, with a smile. "My mom did an ultrasound commercial when she was pregnant with me. And I did some diaper commercials, and it's been *go go go* ever since."

"Oh," I said, impressed. She really did mean she had been acting forever.

"And I spent five years as a minor character on *Lazy Workers*," she said, looking me up and down to see if I recognized her. I didn't, but I nodded enthusiastically anyway.

"So…if you have all this experience…why do you want to audition here?" I asked. "I mean…if you're already a fulltime actress, isn't that a dream come true?"

"Well…" she bit her lip. "It was. But things have been hard since my dad left…and I haven't been able to get much work lately. So my mom thought this would be a good opportunity for me. Plus, *hello*, Liam Swift is the headmaster here." She nodded toward the stage, where we had seen Liam disappear. "He can teach me anything, anytime." She winked at me.

"Sure," I replied. I wanted to ask her more, about what it was actually like to be an actor; how it felt when it was your job and not just something you did because you were so in love with it.

27

What was it like, to act every single day and get paid for it? I was about to open my mouth when the curtain rose. It seemed nothing official was starting quite yet, but Liam and his cronies were on the stage now. The redhead I had seen earlier was standing at the edge of the stage, scanning the crowd. Finally, she turned to him, and nodded.

He stepped forward, clearing his throat. Before he even got to say a word, the lights dimmed and a wave of applause broke out, followed by cheering. Liam glared out into the crowd, waiting for it to settle before he spoke.

"Welcome to the auditions for the scholarship fund. Students who have won the scholarship over the years have gone on to do great things including TV, movies and Broadway. Every second year, we award one person, gender and age not being a factor, and fund them for as long as they need to be at this school— kindergarten through graduation, if need be. This student will have the same rights and privileges as any other student here at the Academy. It's quite the opportunity." He paused for applause. "So hopefully, it's in one of you. You'll each get two minutes to read the script, and then you'll be asked to move on. If the panel likes you, you'll be asked for your contact details outside when you exit. So, let's get started," he said, indicating that the rest of his entourage should head down to where the panel normally sat, in front of the first row, facing the stage. "Rows one and two, come line up. And please, two minutes, and then exit. Nothing more," he said, and then walked away from the microphone, oblivious to the applause.

My heart hammering in my chest, I stood up, forced out of the row by the rest of them. My mind was already turning. *Could I pull this off?* I could at least try, just for experience. I was never going to get it, not with the likes of girls like Alicia in the crowd...but why not try? Just for fun. I had time, especially if it was only two minutes per girl. My lunch break wasn't over for another forty five minutes and there were only twenty girls ahead of me. I could make it and then run back. Besides, Adam wouldn't mind if I was five minutes late. Taking a deep breath, I went to line up against the wall with the rest.

"So," Liam's voice boomed as he spoke into the microphone at the panel table. "Two minutes, one of the judges will read opposite you, and then head over to the left exit. If Porsche asks you to give her your contact info, please do." He waved his hand over to the redhead and I raised an eyebrow at her name, giggling. *Porsche?*

"I'm guessing that's his newest thing then, helping out," Alicia whispered to me. "Lucky."

"Who's first?" Liam asked, silencing us. With a gulp, the first girl stepped forward. I closed my eyes, trying to calm down. This was it, I was trapped, and I had to go through with it. I just hoped I wouldn't make a complete fool of myself.

CHAPTER 3: AMY

I was shaking as I inched closer and closer to the front. Each time a girl read, Alicia would either roll her eyes in disapproval, or shake her head, as if there was no hope left.

"That's Candice Manther," she said, as a new girl approached the panel of judges. "Her resume is about three times the size of mine, and she certainly has a salary from her last show. What the hell is she doing here?"

"Maybe she wants a chance, like everyone else?" I said, shrugging. My hands were clenched in fists, as I tried to control my nerves. "Hey, look, I think I changed my mind…"

"What? No!" Alicia turned around, grabbing me like we had known each other for years. "Don't let the likes of Candice Manther put you off. You deserve a chance just like anyone else."

"Right," I replied. My heart was beating fast, and my mouth had gone dry. Of course I wanted a chance, I wanted to act, and it's all I ever thought of. If Sarah were here now, she'd be bouncing off the walls. But in this crowd, I didn't stand a chance. Not with girls who looked vaguely familiar, girls who already had tons of training and a resume longer than the line up to this audition. Still, as I looked over the script in my hands, I felt myself drawn to the words. Like many others in the line, I began to whisper the words over and over to myself in my head. It was a short script, only a couple of pages, and I quickly identified that it was more about expression and body language than the actual words.

I became so absorbed in the script that I barely noticed how close I was to the front. However, when I heard somebody say "Next!" and there was an awkward silence, I realized that it was my turn.

"Um. Me," I said, moving forward.

The lights were bright, and I could barely see the panel in front of me. Liam looked at me with annoyance and I quickly realized I was standing too far back. Moving forward, onto the masking tape 'X' they had put down, I nervously held my ground. He was staring at me. He could probably see right through me and my lack of training.

"I'll read now," he said, and that surprised me. There had been twenty girls in front of me, and they all had someone else on the panel read opposite them. Liam had not uttered a word...until me?

"Right," I said, folding the script and putting it in my back pocket. He raised an eyebrow.

"You don't need it?"

"No, I, uh...have a good memory," I replied, which was true. I also didn't want him to see how badly my hands were shaking.

"Whenever you're ready then," he said, never taking his sharp eyes off me.

I took a deep breath, closing my eyes as the lines flashed through my mind. And then, opening them to face him square on, I started talking.

"You think I've ever cared what you are?" I said. I surprised myself; the first line of a monologue was always difficult for me. But here it was, flowing through me. The words just spilled through my mouth, almost as if I had nothing to do with them. "I have never cared what you are or what you look like."

"And what kind of future do you think we would have?" Liam snapped, as the Beast to my Beauty.

"I don't care about the future," I said, meeting his eyes. "I came here, prepared to hate you...but all that's changed. All of it. I feel things about you that I have never felt before, not with any man. All of a sudden, the world is real. The fairy tales I'm reading are coming true."

"Are you not frightened?" Suddenly Liam was on his feet, growling at me. "Do you not know what awaits you, if you choose this fate? This life with me?"

"Yes," I said, holding my ground. "You."

There was silence, and internally I panicked, wondering if I had forgotten a line. He stared at me for an impossibly long time, and although it made me incredibly uncomfortable, I tried not to break his gaze. Acting was about looks as much as the words that came out of your mouth, and so I continued to meet his eyes with what I thought was love and support; things I thought Beauty would feel for her Beast. No one said anything for quite a while, and then Liam left the table without another word. Everyone watched as he went over to Porsche and whispered something in her ear.

The girl nodded and then crooked a finger, beckoning me over. I went, in the silence, over to her, as Liam passed me, calling "NEXT!" in that gruff bark that was startling to everyone.

"What's your name?" Porsche asked, when she had taken me out into the hallway. I panicked, thinking I was in trouble, that they had caught me, until I remembered that this was a good thing. Had I actually done well? Out of all the girls who had auditioned so far, he hadn't sent one of them over here yet.

"Amy," I said, and spelled my last name for her. She asked a few more details and then scribbled them down as well, making sure my phone number and email were correct. My heart began to sink when she asked for my experience and resume. Of course,

32

having none, I babbled about my work in the kitchens. Maybe all she wanted to know was that I wasn't a complete spoiled deadbeat teenager who had never had a job? In a last ditch effort, I mentioned my father, and homeschooling, hoping anything I had to offer would help. It was when she asked about my mother's profession that I shook my head and tried to change the subject. Outside of the house, I never talked about my mother. I was afraid that the very few memories I had of her, a scent, a happy feeling, would disappear, if I exposed her to the public. They were my memories, all I had left.

Up close, Porsche seemed very familiar, and finally, when she bent over to pick up the pen she dropped, it clicked in my mind. "Are you a dancer?" I asked, before I could stop myself. "You are, aren't you? You're a ballerina for the Russian National?"

"Yes," she said, with a smile, but offered me no more information. Instead, she instructed me to stand against the wall, taking my picture with a Polaroid camera.

"But why are you here then? Did you retire, like Liam did?"

"Nope." The girl was incredibly tight-lipped on information, and it was leading me to believe that she was dating Liam, in secret. "Now Amy, one more question. Do you have any medical conditions?"

"Uh…" My breath caught in my throat. I put myself through all that only to get caught up with this.

"Lying won't do you any good," Porsche said. "If we take you as a student and don't put it on the insurance, we could get in a lot of trouble. It's not going to affect your chances, we just need to know. What condition do you have?" I was about to lie, but the fact that she asked "*what*" meant that she already knew, somehow.

"I'm HIV positive," I said. Porsche stopped at this suddenly, looking at me with an emotion I couldn't quite read. Judgment? Sympathy? Disgust? "Not from drugs or anything like that. My mom was infected. But I'm fine and I'm healthy and I take all the right pills and the doctor says my chances are good. AIDS isn't a death sentence anymore and…" She waved her hand with a smile, writing it down.

"It's fine, Amy. We just needed to know. Thanks. We may be in touch." She gave me a look to indicate that we were more than done here. I nodded and made my way back to the kitchens. It seemed like days ago that I had left them, even though it was just an hour. I was trembling, although I'm sure it wasn't that noticeable. Still, it took a moment of effort to snap my rubber gloves on.

They had taken my information … that was a good thing, right? And they hadn't thrown me out on the spot when they had found out about my health, so that was also good. Still, I knew I needed to put it out of my mind. There were girls in there who were better than me, and I knew it. I had only seen the first twenty auditions, and there were at least two hundred. There was no way I had a shot.

But I couldn't shake the feeling of hope that I had. I had done well, I knew that. And acting in front of the audience for the first time had given me such an adrenaline rush that I soared my way through the rest of the food prep and was allowed to leave early.

As soon as I was out of the kitchen, I texted Sarah. Her response was immediate.

AAAAAAAAAAAAAAAAAAAAAAAAAAAAAAAA. She replied over and over again. *What was he like? Tell me everything, every moment, every detail.*

He seemed kind of stuck up, as always. Like it was an annoyance to be doing this. I looked up as I crossed the street. When my feet hit the sidewalk again, I continued texting. *It's a tradition his grandfather started, so I guess he felt he had to. Regardless, it was a good experience.*

You should have snuck in and watched the rest of the auditions! Pretended you had to work late. She typed quickly. *Omg, if you get in, I might just have to kill you out of jealousy.*

Dad would kill me. I'm almost home, so I'll catch you later. I sent a smiley face and then slipped the phone into my pocket. I didn't want to think about getting in. I knew I couldn't get my hopes up. So instead, I tried to think of other things, keeping my face blank as I walked in the door.

"Dad?" I called. To my surprise, he appeared immediately from the kitchen, an apron tied around his waist. "Hey. Are you feeling better?"

"Much," he said, and I sniffed the air, smelling succulent tomatoes frying in basil. "How did you like the kitchens for the day? Anything interesting happen?" He looked right at me, and my breath caught in my throat.

"Sure, I got to make fake blood. Much more fun than cutting vegetables all day."

"You see, Amy," he said, as he went to set the table. "It's not a fun job, and you're much too intelligent for it. No glamor at all."

"Right," I said, watching him carefully. "So does this mean that you're going back to work tomorrow?"

"Yes, probably," he replied, turning his back to get the glasses.

35

I sighed inwardly. I was glad that he was feeling better, and indeed, he looked much better than when I left him this morning. But the school was my favorite place in the world, even if it meant being in the kitchen all day long.

Sarah and I had once devised a plan that required me to fail school so that I would have to take a job in the kitchens. However, that lasted about half a day. The hell my father rained down on me when I told him I flunked a test taught me to devise another plan, and quickly.

"Well, that's good," I managed, sitting down as he brought out the food.

"Do you have much homework?" he asked, spooning out spaghetti.

I shrugged. "I probably have a few things I can do, but I've been ahead for a while, so nothing urgent," I said, digging into the food. It was good, but everything seemed so bland and boring since I got out of the audition.

"Well, you should continue to get ahead. You never know what is going to happen." Dad gave me a pointed look, and I nodded, wincing. He was referring to the fact that I might get sick again at any moment. Last semester, I was unable to even sit up enough to work on the computer for a good week. Still, I got it done before the deadline, I always did.

"Sure," I replied, shovelling food into my mouth as quickly as I could. Suddenly, I didn't want to be at the table anymore, or even in the house.

As soon as dinner was over and I had done the dishes, I hurried upstairs, under the pretense of doing homework. Instead, I pulled up my favorite statistics site: www.whatarethechances.com.

What are the chances of getting a job out of 400 more qualified candidates? I typed in, selecting the appropriate drop down menus. And then I waited a moment while it processed.

0.001% was the number that flashed on the screen. I sat back and sighed. Somehow, I thought that my chances were even lower. What I needed to do now was forget about it.

Logging into my school site, I clicked open an assignment and started to mindlessly type. Downstairs, I could hear my father rattling around in the kitchen, and I could still smell the sweet aroma of basil from dinner. Despite myself, a tiny smile formed on my lips. If this was all there was for me, would it be so bad? I didn't think so.

Except for that nagging feeling of the greatest moment of my life—which I had left on the stage today.

Forget it, I told myself, and turned on some Broadway show tunes as I worked. Eventually, singing along to Cats, I did.

CHAPTER 4: LIAM

It always amazed me, the lack of talent that came out for auditions; any auditions, not just our scholarship one. When I was in Hollywood, anyone who had a smidgen of actual talent was light-years ahead of the pretty faces that just showed up with a dream. And when we held open auditions at the school, dear God, it was a nightmare. Even girls who were supposed to have tons of experience could barely convey emotion.

Beside me, turning on the lights as we got back to my apartment, Porsche immediately laid out the choices we had narrowed down. Fifteen girls who had made me raise an eyebrow when they read.

"Did you sense anything in there?" I asked, pouring myself a drink and watching the sun begin to set. She rolled her eyes.

"It doesn't work like that. I can only tell you if a spell is being cast or something, not if there's just a magical being hanging about." She accepted the drink I handed her, and sat down on the couch, her long limbs taking up little space. Still, her position was awkward, and I couldn't help but laugh. Porsche was always folding herself into strange positions, the mark of a true dancer.

She wasn't just a dancer, of course. Although her personality was entertaining, and she knew how to tear up a room, it was more than her talent that had first strung us together.

Three years ago, when I was newly turned and trying to forget, I stumbled upon a high school party, craving blood and death. Just as I felt the cravings were too much, and the entire school was likely to be wiped out, there was Porsche, grabbing my arm, wanting nothing more than to ask the Hollywood star to dance. And suddenly, the cravings were gone.

Porsche was a Shield; a form of supernatural being that was almost legend. There were only three bloodlines left in the world that produced Shields—the Camerons, the McIntoshes, and the most powerful one, her bloodline, the De Ritters. By her touch, she rendered supernatural beings powerless. Witches couldn't light candles, Vampires couldn't intimidate, Werewolves couldn't transform and Ghosts couldn't appear. When she touched me, it was like I never craved anything but pizza and booze.

Not that she had a particular inclination to stop my cravings. She didn't care one way or the other, and encouraged me to *be what you are*, and *cut out the crap*, her other favorite saying. In return for her services, she made me promise one thing, and one thing only. That, when her natural death came, I would transform her into a vampire, and she would get to be immortal.

She wanted to live; to walk in the sun and dance in the rain. And while I saw the value in that argument, it was incredibly stupid, and she knew it. At fourteen, at the wrong kind of party, Porsche had used a dirty needle and contracted HIV. And while she may be managing it fine now, with a good prognosis, all it took was one wrong turn when she was on tour with the Ballet, and she'd be gone, without me to fix it. I had threatened her a hundred times, but with a flicker of those green eyes, she always laughed and walked away. And somehow, I couldn't go against her wishes, not when she had helped me so much. Her blood smelled terrible when I could smell it, and although I fought cravings often, I never wanted her blood. It was infected, broken and unappetizing.

Our friendship wasn't romantic, although I'm sure there had been a drunken night once or twice. Instead, it was full of platonic love and support that I had never found elsewhere.

"So, what are we going to do?" she asked, spreading out the headshots.

I glanced at them, downing my drink. Soon, the sun would disappear, and I would be, as she put it, what I was. I wanted to make this choice while I was still human. "Throw darts and pick one?" I replied, sitting beside her. She thought for a moment, and then pulled one out, handing it to me.

"This one was in Hollywood for a while with you, Candice," She flipped to the back, looking at the resume. "If you wanted good publicity for the school, this one is a good way to go. Shows that the school only takes the best of the best, and even Hollywood is not the best."

"Yeah, no," I immediately discarded her. "She's got money. If she wants to, she can pay her own way. She's just on a power trip, and I won't tolerate it." Setting her headshot aside, I picked up the next one.

"She was good," Porsche said, looking at the headshot of Terry Monroe. "But..."

"She has a lisp," I said, flipping it over to see a lack of resume. "It would take about 4 years of speech training before she could even start acting properly, and that wasn't the point." I smiled as I reached for another one, a six year old girl who would start in our youngest class, and therefore would be mine to shape and mold from the beginning.

"No." Porsche shook her head, folding her long legs up under her. "She's adorable, and anyone will take adorable, her chances are endless."

"Right, but she's six," I pointed out. "I can mold her into whatever I want. She could be a success story from the very beginning; she'd credit everything she ever learned to us. It'll be good for the school."

40

"And when you stand beside an 18 year old at a press conference, looking barely older than you are now, how's that going to work?" Porsche asked, and I shrugged.

"I age."

"You're aging because you're treating your human body like crap," she replied. "That's not aging, that's just looking hung-over every morning."

I grinned at her, even as I got up to fill another drink. And then, I felt my jaw twitch, a sign that my fangs were starting to grow in for the night. Glancing out the window, I saw that it was almost dark.

"Porsche."

"So come sit here and stop being dumb," she replied, holding out her hand. Reluctantly, I went.

The second I touched her, the cravings began to recede. Picking up another picture, I was suddenly transported back to the audition, when this bright-eyed young girl had read with me. I remembered her at once, the way she watched me without awe or fear, the way the words had tumbled out of her mouth naturally.

"That's Amy," Porsche said, her eyes softening. "She's eighteen, which means she'll only have a year, maybe two if she agrees to go back a grade. She doesn't have any experience." Everything she said was negative, yet I heard the softness in her voice. I turned, to meet her eyes.

"So...what then?"

Porsche let go of my hand to flip over the headshot, where notes were scribbled. The second she did, the cravings came back, now that it was fully dark. I could feel my fangs surge forward in my mouth. The sun was set, and my transformation, subtle yet obvious, was complete.

"Amy is also HIV positive," she said, softly. I felt something move in me; a twinge of sympathy for this bright young girl. And she was good; she had blown me and everyone else in the room away. But it was knowing, looking at her as I gritted my teeth against the bloodlust, that she would never tempt me, never be in danger at my hands, and never have to run from the room if a late night rehearsal was needed.

"How?" I asked, standing up to pace the room.

"Her mother was infected, apparently." Porsche looked over the form carefully. "She's homeschooled...or rather, online schooled. Lives with her father, who is not infected. He's employed as a chef at the school, and all of her work experience is also in the kitchens."

"That's right," I remembered now, seeing her face in the hallway more than once. Her father also came to mind: a tall, wirily man, with grey in his hair and an aura of sorrow about him. *If he thought losing his wife was bad, he should try becoming undead and knowing everyone you love will be dead soon enough.* I downed another shot, looking out the window as the town's nightlife began to emerge. It hit me like a hammer, a warm feeling rushing over me. Already, I could feel the effects, the cravings ceasing a bit as the alcohol warmed my blood. That was one problem with being a vampire; I was forever cold, even during the day as a human.

Whoever invented the story that vampires were bloodthirsty creatures all the time was clearly in the mindset of torture and angst. Only turning as the sun set was quite enough for me, I didn't think I could stand for it during the day.

"I want her," I said, turning to Porsche, who was already packing up the other files. I smiled ruefully. The girl knew me too well.

"Fine. I'll put her information into the computer and have her called in the morning."

"I want to call her," I said, surprising her. "Myself."

"If you can remember." She smirked at me, as she finished putting everything away, and then stood up. Clad in leggings, with her red hair piled on top of her head, she looked every bit the successful dancer.

"You going somewhere?" I asked, feeling giddy with drink. "I thought I'd take you out to paint the town red."

"Oh, I see," she replied, smirking, probably at the state I was descending into. "Literally?"

God, she was beautiful. Despite it all, there was something in me that knew that if she wasn't stunning, I probably wouldn't keep her around. That's what you get when you spend years in Hollywood, frolicking with only the beautiful people.

Mind you, that's also what got me into this mess to begin with. But tonight ... tonight I didn't care. We had worked hard for months to pull these auditions together, and now that it was over, and the choice was made, we could relax.

"Literally," I replied, reaching for one more drink. "I want to take my time tonight, find the best of the best. Isn't that what we deserve, after all? So hold my hand, hold me back ..." I started singing and she laughed, heading for the bathroom.

"Ok, hold on, let me try to make myself presentable," she replied. "I have an idea, there's a carnival about two towns over, small little place, but it will be populated with tourists. Everyone will be dressed up, and no one will notice a little chaos..."

"This is why I love you," I said, deciding to make the shot a double. After all, if it was going to be a long drive, I needed to be fortified.

CHAPTER 5: AMY

I knew the bills were overdue, but I realize how badly they were until I woke up the next morning and found that my cell phone was not charged and the lights in my room did not turn on.

"Dad?" I called, hearing his voice in the kitchen as I headed down the stairs. He was on our house phone, furiously arguing and scribbling something onto the back of an envelope. I headed to the stove and switched it on, hoping to make breakfast, but my hopes were quickly killed when the red light remained unlit.

Finally, my father hung up, continuing to write things on the back of the envelope.

"What's going on?" I asked finally, and he sighed.

"We're just...a little behind on things, Amy, that's all. I had the bills set up to be withdrawn automatically, so I wouldn't forget them...but it appears..."

"We don't have enough money," I filled in. "It's not surprising. You're missing a week or more of pay."

"Thank you for reminding me." He glared at me, as I sat at the table, mentally calculating how much we would be missing.

"Dad, let me come today."

"No," he said, sharply. "You missed yesterday, and that was enough. You should stay home, Amy and..."

"Work with an abacus and a pencil and paper?" I asked, unimpressed. "My computer won't turn on, there's no heat in the house, it's Tuesday, so the library is closed, and I can't even use my cell phone." I knew I had a point, so I continued to talk. "So unless I can call into an online school and get all the information faxed over...without a fax machine...it's better that I come with you. I can

45

do homework on the school's wireless, and work for half a day, make up the missing wages faster."

"How are you feeling?" He gave me a long hard look, and I did my best to match it. I felt a bit tired from yesterday, but that was normal.

"Fine," I replied. "It'll only be for half a day. Adam said that I could have a few shifts a week any time. Anything is better than staying here, and the faster we get everything turned back on, the faster I can stay home and rest."

Dad sighed, relenting. "Fine. But if you start to feel overtired at all, you'll come back home right away, agreed?"

"Yep." I shot upstairs, to grab my cell phone, charger and laptop, packing a bag with everything I thought I would need. Of course, I had no intention of doing homework, but I had to create the illusion of doing so. The senior theater class had rehearsal today, and I wanted to catch that. I could charge my phone at the school, keeping Sarah in the loop.

"Are you ready?"

"Yes." Dad was increasingly impatient and I knew that he wasn't happy about the idea of me going to work with him. However, he couldn't argue with my logic, and so off we went, arriving at the school only a few minutes before his shift was due to start.

"Back again?" Adam said, teasing as he saw me. I nodded, but Dad wasn't in the mood for jokes.

"Clock her in for half a day please, Adam, nothing more."

"Aye aye, Captain," he said, making a face at me behind his back. I giggled, as I headed toward the changing room. "We've got more props to cook, Amy, come on over here."

"Yep." If there was one thing I was happy to do without protest, it was that. Adam led me to a corner, where there was a list of food props that the various shows needed. Everything from fake blood to turnip cake. As I was making them, I spent my time wondering what they were for, imagining the scenes and characters they could be useful for. The turnip cake, I imagined, was for a young girl, falling in love, and wanting to bake for her boyfriend. However, she didn't have very much money, and so all she could make him was a turnip cake. The fake blood was for the knife slipping and cutting her hand off on stage, leading her to die a dramatic death, all for love.

I almost cut my own fingers off, imagining this scene, and it made me realize I wasn't paying attention to my work at all.

"A permanent cake?" I looked at the next item on the list. "What's that?"

"That's a prop that is real, but has to last. Maybe a sugar glaze or something," Dad said, looking over my shoulder from where he was preparing lunch for the students. "Those are for Beauty and the Beast next term, it's a feast scene, so we have to get started now in order to have it ready in time."

"Beauty and the Beast?" I asked. The audition suddenly came rushing back to my mind. "Is that what they are doing?"

"It's a media stunt. Liam will play the lead, opposite a senior girl. Looks like he's dying to get back into acting." Dad rolled his eyes.

"Right," I replied, looking at the list. There were several pages of what I thought were instructions, but were actually a list of

47

props. "Wow, there's a lot of food to cook. This will take me until next term for sure."

"No, it will take *us* until next term," he said. "*You'll* be doing homework and preparing for college."

"Right," I mumbled, heading for the ingredients cupboard. Liam was playing Beast? That'd be interesting indeed. Especially the scene where the Beast becomes a prince. Despite his attitude, I couldn't deny Liam was handsome, nor could I deny his talent. There was so much to learn from him, so much talent in just his little finger. Whoever got to play his Beauty would be a lucky girl indeed.

My luck—as small as it was—held out when Dad allowed me to go to work with him again the next day … and again the day after. I was showing him I could do my school work, work, and even sneak off to a theater class or two, without issue. Every day, I checked my email, but found no audition results notice, so slowly, hope shrunk from my thoughts. I assumed if they couldn't reach me through my cell phone, which had been suspended by the phone company, they would email, but there was nothing. And I knew that the first rule of acting was never to seem too eager, so I didn't inquire. It was probably safe to assume that I wasn't getting the part. I was, somehow, alright with this conclusion. The experience that I had gotten, the warm feeling of fulfillment when I stood in front of all those people, was enough to keep me afloat for years to come. It was a dream come true, to read those lines in front of a live audience—and with Liam, even though I didn't admit it to anyone but myself.

<u>CHAPTER 6: LIAM</u>

"Still no answer."

I almost growled at the secretary as I came out to check on the status of our scholarship recipient. It was Friday, and we still hadn't gotten in contact with her. Typical Porsche had left me unable to read her handwriting, and so Amy's email address was illegible. The phone number was all we had, and it rang constantly, without a voicemail.

"I'm going to go down to the kitchens and get something to eat," I said, as calmly as I could manage. "And then when I come back, we'll contact the runner up."

The secretary nodded, and I stalked off, pulling out my cell phone as I walked.

Any idea who I should pick as a second choice? I texted Porsche, checking my watch. She had flown back to Russia for a charity ball. The ballet was supposed to be on break now, but occasionally, there was a gig or two she had to attend. The time difference said it was early evening, so she should be able to answer me.

Why??? She texted back instantly. I thanked my stars that she was often glued to her phone. Looking down as I typed, I pushed open the doors to the kitchen. This was a modern mishap, something I guess I had to learn to deal with if I was going to live forever. I collided head on with somebody, who let out a startled yelp that was followed by a clatter of kitchenware.

"Sorry," I said, barely looking up.

"No problem," Amy replied, and I stood, shell-shocked, staring at her.

"You're here."

"Uh…huh." Quickly, she glanced behind her, to her father, who was approaching.

"Headmaster. Is there something we can get you?"

"Yes!" I said, probably with a bit too much excitement. Both of them had mirror image expressions such that you could see the family resemblance. "Your daughter."

"Excuse me?" he asked, shocked.

"Amy tried out at our open auditions for the full scholarship. We selected her and have been trying to get in contact, but…"

Suddenly, without warning, the young girl pitched forward. My reflexes were faster than a human's, and I spent many a night at parties catching those who couldn't hold their liquor.

Deadweight was always heavier than it looked, and I decided that the easiest course of action was to ease onto the floor with her, her limp body already rejoining the world of the conscious.

There was commotion in the kitchen, as everyone rushed toward her, calling her name, trying to decide if they should call for an ambulance. Her father went tearing into the changing room, I assumed to find her bag of tricks. Even now, in my human form, I could tell this girl had something off about her.

Her eyelids fluttered and she came to, staring straight up at me. She really was beautiful, when she wasn't nervous, her face symmetrical and angular, her eyes piercing and huge, reminding me of a baby deer. Her lips were full and soft, and I couldn't help but wonder what it would be like to kiss her.

"Are you alright?" I asked, softly, under the commotion, and she nodded, trying to make sense of her surroundings.

"Amy!" Her father came sliding back onto the scene, almost ripping her away from my arms. He shoved a white pill into her hand, and while she looked annoyed, she swallowed it, dry.

"Dad, I'm alright. I'm alright. I was just…surprised. Ladies used to swoon all the time in the middle ages." She tried to smile, leaning half against her father and half against a table leg. "Am I really the one you chose?"

"What's this about?" her father demanded, looking at me as if I was the one who caused her to faint. Which, to be fair, I guess was true.

"Our open call for a full scholarship, room and board. Lots of girls tried out, but Amy was the one who showed the most promise."

"Is this a joke?" His eyes narrowed. "Amy may be talented, but she has never had a formal education in theater."

"All the more reason for her to go to a formal school for theater education," I replied, raising an eyebrow. Behind me, a few of the chefs chuckled in spite of themselves. "All of her costs will be taken care of for the time she is educated with us. We're prepared to start her as a junior if she goes back a grade or a senior if she wants to remain here just for the remainder of her education. You are homeschooled, Amy?"

"Yes." She nodded, still in shock.

"Then we'll have to give you a few tests to see where you are."

"Amy is educated properly, I promise you," her father said, and I shrugged.

"I didn't say she wasn't." I began to realize how silly it was that we were having this entire conversation on the floor. Shifting slowly, I pushed myself up, reaching a hand to Amy, who took it. I pulled her up as well, while her father used the table for support. "Now, I came in here for some lunch," I said, trying to brush off the dramatics of the situation. "And then, after that, if you wish, you two can meet me in my office and we can discuss the particulars, if you accept."

"I accept!" Amy blurted out, and her father gave her a sharp look.

I sighed, plucking a readymade sandwich from a tray, and headed toward the door. Before I pushed it open, I looked back, attempting to make my comment seem offhand "Of course, the scholarship would include full medical insurance, as all our students buy into it." I didn't stay to hear their reaction, but continued walking down the hall. I knew that it would be the deciding factor in the end. In acting, they called it *changing tactics*, shifting from one point to the next, until you get what you want. And I knew I had just won.

Pulling out my phone, I sent a quick text to Porsche, who was probably going out of her mind with curiosity.

Never mind...

Immediately, it beeped:

(#$(#$(#($*!@@#$!!!

Came the reply, and I laughed, as I shut the door to my office. It was good to know I could still drive her nuts across the ocean.

CHAPTER 7: AMY

I had never seen my father so angry as he was that afternoon. When lunch time came, he clocked me out with such a glare that I dared not argue. And then, he clocked himself out for break, took my arm, and marched me down the hall. When we found an empty classroom, he practically shoved me in and closed the door firmly behind him.

"Explain yourself, Amy. You have 10 seconds."

"It's exactly what Liam said. I know we've talked about this before, and it's always been about money. But when I saw the lineup, and heard about the scholarship…I just thought I'd try, what harm was there in that? I don't know why he chose me, over a thousand other girls with longer resumes, but he did … and Dad, it's a full scholarship. Everything's covered, including the medical bills. And you're here every single day, so if something goes wrong, you'll be here. Heck, we'll spend more time together now because we won't be apart for 10 hours while you are at work. I'll be here, right down the hall. It's only for a year, Dad, and colleges prefer if you have a diploma from a school that actually exists in the physical realm and…" I was babbling and probably very close to crying as well. Dad still hadn't said a word to me, and when I stopped for breath, silence engulfed the room. "Please say something."

He sighed. "Is this what you really want, Amy?"

"Yes!" I cried, frantic. "Yes, this is what I really want, more than anything. And I promise, if I start to feel sick or anything goes wrong, I'll tell you right away! You can come check on me every break and we can have dinner in my dorm room and I'll come home every weekend, I swear…."

"Amy," He waved his hand, looking tired. "If you really want this, then I'll support you. You're right, all your reasons have been right." He looked at me with a sad smile. "How did I ever raise such a bright girl?"

I couldn't believe my ears. "Really?"

He grinned. "Really," he said, and I flew into his arms, hugging him.

"Thank you, Dad! Thank you!"

He laughed, squeezing me tight before pulling me to face him.

"All right, I only have forty five minutes left, so we should go speak to the headmaster, yes?"

I nodded, letting him lead the way to the headmaster's office.

When we got there, the secretary let us right in, clearly knowing why we were there. Liam was at his desk, feet propped up, and munching on the sandwich he had taken. When he saw us, he threw his arms up.

"*Hallelujah*, the missing child returns."

"I'm sorry." I blushed. "My cell phone was...broken."

"And your email was written down wrong," he said, and then shrugged, pulling his feet off the desk. "Have a seat, you two. I have the paper work right here. Any questions?" He put a large stack of papers in front of Dad, who looked daunted by them.

"...Everything is covered?" he asked, and Liam nodded, ticking things off on his fingers.

"Tuition, room and board, medical insurance and spending money."

"Spending money?" I looked up, surprised. Liam shrugged.

"Part of the tuition fees we ask for is so the students can have an allowance every week for items they may need. You'll receive one hundred every week."

I nearly fell off my chair. It got better and better.

"Now...Amy does have a medical condition..." Dad started. "And I trust if anything happens, I'll be called immediately...and allowances will be made for her health?"

"Dad!" I said, embarrassed.

Liam's eyes met mine, with tenderness that surprised me. This was the first time I had seen him emote something that wasn't arrogance or anger. He nodded. "Yes, of course. I will personally see to it. I have a close friend with the same condition, so I do have experience in the matter."

"Oh." Dad seemed to be out of questions, and so he opened the folder, scrawling his initials where requested.

My head was spinning, watching him. I couldn't believe that this was actually happening. Right here, right now.

"Amy, why don't we take a tour of the school?" Liam leapt to his feet suddenly. "We'll leave your father to read all this, and by the time we come back, we can answer any questions he may have."

"Sure," I said, trying not to let on that I already knew the school like the back of my hand. I stood up as well, leaving my bag on the floor, and followed him out the door.

"We'll start with the senior wing, as that's where you'll be," he said, looking quickly down the deserted hallways, and then turning to the left.

"When will I start?" I asked, and he shrugged.

"That's up to you. You can wait until next term if you wish, but ideally you can start…"

"Tomorrow?" I asked, and he laughed, giving me a warm smile.

"Sure. If you want."

I was surprised how well we got on, one on one. When I met him before, he didn't strike me as the type to joke around. But now that we were alone, it was like his guard was dropping.

We walked past several classrooms, poking our heads in as Liam described the subjects taught there. Eventually, we got to the theater, which was full of people.

"This is where you'll be next term, for Beauty and the Beast," he said, and suddenly, the conversation in the kitchens came rushing back.

"You'll be Beast, won't you?" I asked, and he nodded.

"Acting is an addiction, Amy, and I thought it'd be good for the school to have some publicity as well. All press is good press." He gave me a rueful smile. "Besides, I miss being on stage. It's where I got my start."

"Right." I nodded, and took a deep breath, straightening up. "Let's keep going."

Liam grinned, and waved his hand, indicating our direction. Soon, we crossed the barrier between the senior and junior doors, and I found myself in a sea of giggling young children, about to be let out for recess. I had never been in this part of the school, because sneaking in would have looked way too suspicious at my age. Even when I was younger, it was easier to pretend to be someone's kid sister watching a rehearsal than be part of a small class where the teacher knew everyone's name. Liam smiled as the kids giggled.

"This is the best age to start young actors, really. Every single one of these children acts without thinking. They don't put method or thought into it; they do it because it feels right in their gut and they say their lines as if it's the first time. If only all of us could remember that," he said, and I found myself swept away by the tenderness in his face as he watched them.

"But that's how you act," I pointed out. "In the movies. I always believed that you were whatever character you were playing. It never felt fake."

"Thank you." He gave me a smile as we walked through the hallways.

"But I can see how so many classes and rehearsals could interfere with the way somebody acts." I kept going, speaking before I even really thought properly. "I mean, you could spend so much time thinking about the method and the training that you forget to just...be the character and exist." I was babbling and I knew it, but he smiled at me.

"That's why I chose you, Amy. So many of these students here are trained to the point of robots. Most of them won't have a future. But you read those lines as if you were Beauty, and nothing else around you mattered. If you can hold on to that naturalism, you will have a future in the industry."

"Why did you leave?" I asked, suddenly. "I mean...you had a future?"

His face clouded over and he shook his head, his jaw clenching. I saw that familiar look that he wore as he often strode through the halls.

"It doesn't matter," he said, and pushed open another door. It led to the front of the school, where there was a separate theater, newly built in the former parking lot. Just as we were crossing the pavement, I heard someone call his name.

"Liam!"

He swore, and I realized it was a cameraman, approaching fast. Apparently, having left Hollywood or not, the paparazzi were always around. It made sense. He had been one of the biggest movie stars on the planet. And on top of that, many of the students had careers and TV credits that brought them some sort of fame outside the school. If the paparazzi wanted a photo of something, they had a good chance of getting it just by hanging around the front doors.

"Not now, please," he said, barely turning around and taking me by the arm. He was increasing his pace toward the theater and I was struggling to keep up. "I'm trying to teach."

"What's your name?" the photographer called to me. I turned, gaping, and looked at Liam, who sighed and then shrugged.

"You know what? Fine. This is Amy, our full scholarship winner for this year. Amy was the best, out of thousands of hopefuls, and she and I will be playing opposite in Beauty and the Beast next term. That's right, she and I." He glared at the cameraman. "So take that, and write it in your paper, and publish a pretty photo, and if you give us so much as one out of focus picture or subpar review, I will make sure you are banned from school property and never get another picture again."

And with that, Liam pulled me toward the new theater.

"Bloody leeches," he said, shaking his head. "Always dying for a piece of drama."

I felt like I was going to faint again, Liam's words spinning in my head.

"I'll be Beauty?" I said, and he met my eyes.

"Well, you'll be my Beauty, of course. It was always going to be the scholarship winner, providing she was old enough."

I leaned against the wall, and concern clouded his face.

"Are you alright? Do you need anything?" He bent to my level, a gentle hand on my shoulder.

"Something to eat maybe?"

I flushed bright red at the attention, and shook my head. "No, you just surprised me. I've never acted before, you know that, right? And you're..."

"Amy, I promise I'll work with you every step of the way," he said. "Every actor is only as good as his partner."

"But won't the other students be angry? The ones who have been here longer?"

He laughed at that, shaking his head. "No. One of the lessons we teach here is that there are so many variables when getting a part, including things you can't control. Don't worry about them."

"That's easy to say until they eat me," I said, and he laughed at that, a slow and easy laugh that made me join him.

"The only one you have to worry about eating you is me, if you become delinquent," he said, leading me toward the stage.

"What...uh...paper did he work for?" I asked, indicating the paparazzi that we left outside. Liam smiled.

"Your first piece of fame. Of many, I think. Don't worry, I'll find out and get you a few copies."

"Thanks," I replied, looking around the stage. I couldn't believe all of this was happening, that it was actually real. "I didn't want all of that, though. I mean, it's cool, but it doesn't matter."

"What do you mean?" he asked, intrigued.

"It's just...it's stupid, you're going to laugh," I blushed, but he took a step forward, cocking his head with interest.

"No, please, tell me."

"When I was a kid, I used to memorize monologues and do them in my room. Nowadays, I put them on YouTube. I used to sit in on classes here, sneak around."

"I surely would have noticed you," he replied, giving me a flattering smile. I grinned.

"I'm good. I'm sneakier than the Phantom of the Opera."

"Indeed you are, for if I had seen you before, there's no way I could have ignored you." He was close to my face, standing only a few feet apart. If it were any other stranger who did that, I would have felt awkward and uncomfortable about it. But with Liam, I strangely felt relaxed.

"I would watch the classes, or the rehearsals, whatever was going on. And before you found me in the kitchen...I was content with the fact that the audition would be the happiest moment of my life, being up there and acting like that. I can't imagine film is that good, is it?"

"As good as theater?" He was still smiling, and his eyes were twinkling. "No, but the money's better."

"I don't care about the money." I shrugged. "I grew up poor, and I haven't dropped dead yet, so money doesn't matter. But being up there, in a room buzzing with energy, and everyone's eyes on you, watching you perform. Feeding off their energy. Just—wow…"

Liam laughed and I blushed harder.

"See, I'm a nerd. You laughed."

"No, no, Amy." He shook his head, his eyes intense. "I wasn't laughing at you. I was just amused by the fact that you seemed to read my mind. Film was good, the fame and money were nice…But I never felt more alive than when I was on a stage. I wished I could have stayed in that profession forever, just only on stage, without any of the crap that came with Hollywood."

"Oh…" I paused. "But…now…"

"But just living changes us a lot," he managed, and I nodded.

"Of course. But now you're Beast, so you'll be on stage again. So you're happy, right?"

He nodded, taking my arm and leading me to the next place on our tour.

"Yes, Amy, I believe I can be happy again."

I couldn't wait to go home and text Sarah, now that I'd have the money to turn my cell phone back on. If I couldn't believe it and I was standing right there, I could only imagine how she was going to feel.

I smiled, despite myself. Never in a million years had I dreamt this would happen; if someone told me what my life would be like three years ago, I would have laughed in their face. My life was the same old routine day in and day out. But now, life was finally taking shape and all because I wandered down the wrong hallway.

CHAPTER 8: AMY

I was so excited for the first day of school, I could hardly sleep. My father had quickly squashed the idea of moving in the next day, but between Liam and me, I won the battle to move in over the following weekend. And now, here I was, the last of my stuff packed in boxes to move to the dorms. Classes would start tomorrow for me, but a dorm had been reserved so that every day on his way to work, Dad could carry a box or two and drop it off for me. My online course credits had all been sent to the school, and transferred in. I would be a senior in every course with the option to return for partial credits next year in the theater department if I needed to. The school admitted students all-year round and offered courses all-year round as well, so I wouldn't be as out of place as I thought I would be. Their schedule was dependent on the shows they were producing and touring (in freshman year, they toured the Islands for three months which had made me jealous to no end), and so admitting students according to the needs of the theater had become standard.

"Do you want to take those today?" Dad asked, appearing in the doorway of my room. "Or shall I bring them tomorrow for you?"

"Um…" I turned to him, standing in the middle of my now empty room. "I thought I could move today. That way, I could get a good night's sleep and go right to class tomorrow…"

"Oh," he replied. "If that's what you want…"

"Dad," I said, trying to smile. "We'll see each other MORE now than we did before. It's going to be fine, I promise. If anything, I'll be safer because you spend all day just down the hall from me."

"I know." He nodded, but his eyes were still sad. "I'll just miss you."

"You won't have a chance to miss me." I grinned. "I'll bother you every moment of the day."

"I hope so." He gave me a firm hug, not letting go for more than a minute. Finally, he stepped back. "You want to go by yourself and unpack, don't you?"

I nodded.

"I'll be back for dinner. I promise. I just want to get a feel of the place."

"All right," he said, and reached into his pocket, handing me the keys. "It's room 66, on the 6th floor."

"Great." I put them in my purse, picked up the last box and a bag and kissed him on the cheek. "See you at dinner."

I had only ever snuck into the dorms once before, and it was years ago. There was a double door at the front that required two keys, and then a key to each floor as well as your own dorm room key. So nothing prepared me for the beauty I was met with when I entered the lobby.

On all sides of the security desk were murals; stunning and colorful and ceiling high. In seemingly random, yet perfect spots were headshots and photographs of students and productions long past, staring back at me with contented eyes and happy smiles. I instantly felt at home and comfortable. So at home, in fact, that I walked right by the desk without checking in.

"Excuse me!" a girl called out to me as I walked by, and I turned, sharply. "Do you live here?"

"Uh...I'm new, but yes? I think so?" I replied.

She smiled, reaching out her hand. "I'm Sheena."

"Amy," I said, carefully juggling my load to shake it. "I'm uh...I don't know where I'm going."

"Are you a senior?" she asked brightly, and I nodded. "And what course stream are you?"

"Uh..." I paused. "I'm the scholarship winner?"

"OH!" Her eyes lit up. "You're the winner. Congrats then! You're in the theater wing. Do you have your room number? I can take you."

"Sure." I handed her my key, and she started down the hall. "What uh...other wings are there?"

"That's the dance wing, there," she said, pointing down one hall way. "And the musical wing is that one, off to the left. And then the technical wing, for all things not on stage." She pointed to a hallway behind her. "It's more for organizational purposes, you know ... like all the dancers can easily have a meeting in their common room, and all the actors can have rehearsal in their hallway. It's not really cliquey or anything, we all hang out all the time and we all take some cross-stream classes." She was leading me toward an elevator, which opened with my key. Getting inside, she pressed the 6th floor button. "The higher you go, the older the students are. Makes it easier for the dorm mothers to manage. You're on the second highest floor—the one above you is more of a hotel, reserved for visiting artists and such."

"What's your story?" I asked, and she gave me a sad smile.

"I came here when I was six, as a dancer. But when I was fifteen, I injured my IT band and killed my career."

"Oh!" My eyes widened. "I'm so sorry."

"That's ok." She shrugged. "It happens to a lot of dancers. I spent a few years abroad and then came back here, and took a job managing this place. It makes me feel like I'm involved again. Here we are."

The elevator opened to a crowd of giggling girls, who greeted Sheena and then got in as we exited.

"Hey, Tammy, there's a package for you at the front desk," Sheena called, and the girl called Tammy nodded, as the doors closed and we continued down the hallway. "And, 66." She popped the key in the door, and opened it.

I gasped when I saw the inside of my room. There was a bed, a kitchen and a bathroom all crammed into a small space to make room for the living room. It held a barre running against one wall, with floor to ceiling mirrors, and hardwood floors. There was a bureau with lights around the mirror, and an extensive makeup kit, as well as a large closet with every type of hanger you could imagine. The lights in the room were all on dimmer switches that looked more complicated than some theater soundboards.

"Even when you sleep, you practice. All the rooms look like this. No one ever has an excuse to not work," Sheena said, with a smile. My stuff was all in the center of the living room floor waiting to be unpacked. "Need anything else?"

"No, thanks," I said, still looking around the room in awe.

"All right, well, if you need me, I'm just a phone call away. It's #1 on the phone." She pointed to a houseline on the desk, and then gave me a smile, and left.

Alone in the room, I began to pull my stuff out of boxes, folding it carefully to fit in the drawers and cupboards. This place was bigger than my room at home, and I knew it was going to look sparse when I was done. However, it was my place and the very thought of that sent chills down my spine.

"Knock, Knock!"

I turned, startled, to find Liam at my door.

"Liam!" I said, before I could stop myself. "Er...I mean...Mr. Swift."

"Liam is fine," he said, leaning against the doorway with a smirk. "They told me you were finally moving in, and I wanted to make sure you had your class schedule for tomorrow."

"Sure." I said, looking at the desk where I had unfolded it. "I have Shakespeare in the morning and then Theater History right after it. In the afternoon, there's a whole block to be in the senior theater."

"Sounds right," he said, watching me unpack. "There should be a script for a practice show in one of your drawers. I want you to go over it before tomorrow, if you have time. We won't perform it in full, but we'll take it to a workshop level in class."

"Right," I said, looking up at him. I couldn't believe how fast my heart was beating. Here I was, standing a few feet away from one of the biggest movie stars on the planet (or at least, he used to be), and about to start theater school.

"I brought you this." He reached into his back pocket and pulled out a newspaper. My eyes widened as I recognized our picture on the front.

"Oh wow!" I couldn't stop myself from ripping it from his hands, and he laughed at my excitement.

"Your first tabloid cover," he said, watching as I read it. They didn't have much information on me, but it had paragraphs about past scholarship winners, including, to my surprise, a familiar name.

"Porsche De Ritter had a dance scholarship here?" I asked, looking up at him. He grinned at the mention of her name.

"She did. Took it right out from under thousands of hopefuls, stayed three months, and then was recruited to the Russian National Ballet. Please stay longer than three months," he said, turning his megawatt grin on me. I was surprised by this personality that was emerging from Liam. All the other times, I had seen him, he was emotionless; his jaw set, barking orders at people. But now, alone in my room, he was showing me his sense of humor and a laid back side of him I never would have guessed. I was flattered that he would even bother to come check in on me, when there were hundreds of students in this school. But still, there he was.

"If you'll have me," I managed. There was a silence then as we stood, simply looking at each other. Since the first day that I met eyes with Liam, I felt like we knew each other from before. His eyes were so full of expression and soul that it was overwhelming. I felt comfortable, simply being there with him.

"I'll see you in class then, tomorrow, unless you need anything else?" he finally said, breaking the gaze and I nodded.

"I'm going back home for dinner, and then I'm sleeping here tonight. So...unless you wanted to talk to me tonight?"

I was asking innocently, there seemed to be so many things I needed to be caught up on. However, Liam's face instantly darkened and he shook his head.

"No, I won't be free tonight. If you have any questions, you can call Sheena at security." He turned on his heel, suddenly, and was gone before I could stop him.

I sat at the desk, my mind whirling at what I possibly could have said wrong. I hadn't meant to offend him, of course, and I couldn't imagine how I had. Somehow, I must have managed.

Losing my motivation to unpack, I went to put my coat back on. I had never lived alone before, and it was certainly going to be lonely. At that moment, a small part of me wanted nothing more than to head home, see my father for dinner and sleep in my own bed. But that life was over.

CHAPTER 9: AMY

The first week of classes were a blur to me; a constant stream of people and text books; lines and instructions; hallways and colors. Unlike simply sitting in the classes and auditing them, I actually had to participate, to do the work, and answer questions. More than once, I found myself lost trying to find a small classroom, or backstage entrance. The students were helpful, friendly for the most part and willing to share their textbooks and scripts with me until I got my own ... at least in the beginning. But as time went on, it was Liam who gave me the support I needed, making sure I had time to find my way and pausing to offer definitions of terms or words that must have obviously confused me. And soon, I found the friendly looks from others turning to raised eyebrows, and snickering; dirty glares that would have stopped even the hardest heart in their tracks.

I told myself he was just being nice. He was helping me out. After all, we were to perform together soon, and so we had to work together. I even tried telling the others that. But soon, I found being at school was not much different than being at home. I was isolated, alone and different. The walls were thin, and I could hear a lot through them. I was used to sleeping in pitch darkness and dead silence. But at school, with the hall light constantly on, and the thin walls, I got neither.

It's just that...I don't know. Maybe I'm so useless and need all this extra attention, so they are frustrated with me. And my lack of talent. I texted Sarah one evening, as I sat in one of the common rooms alone. I was supposed to be writing out a modern day translation of a Shakespeare verse, but I found myself unable to focus.

Are you kidding? They're jealous. She replied back instantly. *You beat out a million girls for a scholarship, you're awesome and gorgeous, and the hot movie star/headmaster is paying attention to you. Why are you sad?! This is the ride of your life!*

Maybe he thinks I'm so useless that I'm 'special. I replied back, sullenly. *And that's why he has to stop every five seconds to tell me what something means.*

Video chat. Now. Came the reply, and I sighed. I didn't really have an excuse to say no to her, now that I was at school with free unlimited Wi-Fi. Our video chats could go on for hours without me worrying about our Internet bill. I hit the screen share button and waited for her camera to load up, holding the phone up to my face.

Sarah was pretty, in a kind of exotic way. Her hair was cropped short, in a style I never dared to try, and she always wore eye shadow that made her almond-shaped eyes pop. Up in Canada, she was a community theater actor, being forced by her parents to study finance in university. However, that didn't stop her from dressing like Madonna and auditioning for everything she could find. She had spunk and an energy about her that I always envied.

"You know what you should do?" she said, as soon as her face popped up. Sarah had a liquid French accent that I imagined made every man around her want her. "Take me on a tour of your school. The Wi-Fi goes all over, right?"

"Nooo," I whined, leaning back in my chair. "It's getting dark and I want to go to bed."

"But you'll just lie in bed for hours. Besides, it's like 8pm, Amy, you're acting like a 50 year old."

"Hey." I grinned at that, struggling to my feet. "I have a disease, you know."

"There's the disease...and then there's just you," Sarah teased me. "Or you can sit here and tell me how gorgeous Liam is." I sighed, and hit the button for the rear camera, so she could see things from my point of view.

"All right, fine." I stood up, heading out into the hallway. "But if I get in trouble for illegally filming or something, I'm sending them to arrest you too."

"Show me Liam!" Sarah said to me, and I rolled my eyes, quickly turning the camera around and pulling my headphones out of my pocket, so the whole corridor wouldn't hear her outbursts.

"Sarah, *hush*," I said, burning with embarrassment. "I don't know where he is, geez."

"I thought he was always with you?" she teased, and I rolled my eyes. "Ooo, what's that?"

"That's the dance studio for the juniors," I said, putting the phone up to the window. It was empty, but she could still see the barre decorated with Disney characters and the multi-colored lights.

"Wow. You could have had so much fun as a kid," Sarah said, as I continued to walk, angling the camera to show her various pictures or sticking it into classrooms so she could see my daily environment. I was just about to see if the theater was open when I was distracted by the sudden sound of breaking glass. Sarah must have seen my eyes dart away, because she leaned forward.

"What?"

"Hold on a second," I said, walking carefully toward the sound. *Curiosity killed the cat,* my father always used to tell me. However, I ignored his voice ringing in my ears as I peeked around the corner to the classroom.

"LIAM! Oh my God!" Sarah almost deafened me with her scream. I gave the phone a quick glare, wincing. Sure enough, inside the classroom was Liam, standing in the middle and waving his arms. Porsche sat on a desk, glaring at him.

"She's my Sire, Porsche, darling, she's the one who made me. You expect me to just forget she even existed?"

"I'm just saying be careful," she replied. "You're splashing your face all over the media again, and if she wants to find you, she's going to find you and then this is going to start all over again."

"What are they talking about?" Sarah hissed in my ear. I glanced at her video and angrily put a finger to my lips.

"Let her." Liam shrugged. "There isn't anything that bloodsucker can do to me that she hasn't already done. Not with you around anyway."

The conversation made little sense to me, and made me lean in further, trying to understand exactly what they were talking about. My head crossed a light, and my shadow played strongly against the wall. The change in light was what gave me away. In an instant, they both turned to look at me. I felt the color rise in my cheeks, and I yanked my headphones out.

"Sorry!" I said, quickly. "I was just showing my friend around." I held up the video call on my phone which showed Sarah gaping. Quickly, I ended the call, without saying goodbye.

"Amy!" Liam said a bit too loudly. He looked different from this morning; paler, and more defined in the face and his voice sounded different as well, although I couldn't place it. However, with one whiff of the air in the room, it was probably a safe bet to assume he was drunk. I recognized the smell of brandy from the kitchen ... sweet and potent. "It's ok, the more the merrier."

"Liam," Porsche growled, from her place on the desk. "I think Amy should head back to her dorms, right now."

"Why?" He turned to her, a bit unsteadily. "She's the best student in the school. She's the only one that gives a damn about acting. The rest of them are after fame and fortune. Why shouldn't she stay and join us?"

My mouth hit the floor at his words, which had no trace of sarcasm or untruth in them. He spoke them from his heart, obscured by alcohol as they were. And then he stumbled, reaching to a nearby desk for support. Without thinking, I moved forward, even though I was too far to catch him. I heard it before I felt it; the crunch of glass beneath my feet that speared right through my thin sandal and into my skin. It pierced deep and I cried out from the pain, stumbling forward in alarm. I put my arms out to catch myself but panicked when I realized there was broken glass everywhere.

Liam grabbed me before I fully hit the ground, pulling me out of harm's way before I could do too much damage to my skin. He had moved across the room at seemingly inhuman speed, grabbing me around the waist and pulling me to the left, so we both fell.

For a moment, I was in his lap, his strong arms around me, and I didn't want to move, my heart beating so fast I thought it might explode. But then I felt the rush of blood as my muscles recovered from the fall, and I twisted, trying to get out of his grasp.

"Let go. Let Go. Please let go," I cried, trying to assess where the blood was, and whether any of it had gotten on him. If he had even a drop of blood in any wound, in his face, there was a good chance he could be infected. Liam looked shocked at this, and released me, but soon, I had another problem.

Porsche was in front of me then, grabbing my wrists to get me to stop struggling.

"Amy, are you ok?"

"Please," I said, surprised as tears sprung to my eyes. I had to make her understand. "Please, don't touch me, NO!" I moved my arm away as she reached for it, sprouting blood from broken glass. "I'm HIV positive, my blood is infected. You can't be anywhere near me. You need gloves!"

"Ssh, honey," her voice was gentle as she met my eyes. "Me too."

That stopped me, and I stared at her. She was so beautiful, so healthy, and strong. How could she possibly be infected as well?

"Really?"

"Yep," she said, with a sad smile, as she reached to examine my arm. "Years ago. Dirty needle." She winced as she looked at the wound. "This is going to need the first aid kit. I'm going to get it." She stood up, looking at Liam, who had backed up a bit to lean against a desk. "You alright? I'll be fast."

"Sure." He seemed a bit more sober now, although his eyes weren't as intense as they normally were. "Go ahead, Porsche, I'm not going to eat her."

"Uh huh." The dancer seemed unamused, and headed off down the hallway, breaking into a jog when she got a few feet away. Curling my knees against my chest, I turned to look at Liam. He was looking right back at me, sympathy playing across his face.

"Are you alright?" he asked me, and I nodded.

"Yes, I was just careless."

"If anyone was careless tonight, it was me," he said, sitting down beside me.

"Are you alright?" I cocked my head at him. "You look...sorry, you look terrible."

He laughed, glancing up at the clock.

"It's just time for me to go to bed," he said, and I raised an eyebrow at that.

"A former Hollywood party boy wanting to sleep at 9pm?"

His face darkened at that again, and I saw his mouth twitch. I blinked twice, trying to clear my head. His teeth were white and perfect inside his mouth, but tonight they looked almost menacing.

"There are things the darkness does to me that you don't know, Amy. Things that you don't want to know."

I would have laughed at that, but there was something about the tone in his voice that made me lean closer, my chest tight with empathy.

"Like what?"

He waved his hand, dismissingly.

"We all have our demons in the dark. I'm sorry that you have to...see me like this. The booze helps, believe it or not. But then, you're 18 and young, you should believe it." He gave me a wry smile, and I shrugged.

"I've lived a pretty boring life." I said, quietly, pulling at a thread on my shirt. "But Liam..." There was something about his face, the way he was almost folded in on himself, looking so vulnerable, that made me continue to speak. "You've given me so much help while I've been here. You've given me everything. A year ago, I never would have even dared to dream my life would be like this. So..." I trailed off, meeting his dark eyes. "If there's anything I can do to help you...I know it's not my place, but..." What stopped me this time was what I thought I saw in his eyes; the tears welling up as he spoke, shaking his head.

"You're a good kid, Amy. You shouldn't be mixed up in all this."

"I'm not a kid," I said, immediately, and he met my eyes, a tender smile on his face. He raised a hand to my cheek, and I let him touch it gently.

"Indeed you are not," he said. "You are a beautiful young woman and any man would be blind to refuse you."

I was lost in his eyes, their watery depths flooding into my soul. I had seen his face a thousand times, on the screen and in the magazines, and I couldn't believe it was now inches from mine. Slowly, his other hand rose to my other cheek, and he dipped his head. Without even realizing what was happening, I kissed him.

His lips were soft, and gentle, our tongues chasing each other as our kiss deepened. It seemed to last an eternity, and yet when we broke apart, it wasn't long enough. I gripped onto him and our lips met again, our breath now coming in gasps. I felt things I had never felt before, my skin lit up and a warm glow ignited between my legs. Liam seemed equally entranced, his eyes closed, and his hands began wandering my body. I didn't have time to think, to consider what was happening. All I knew was that I wanted more, and I pulled myself closer to him, remaining careful to keep my wounds away. He tasted of brandy and sweetness, and the way he sucked on my lower lip made me moan.

Finally, we broke apart, our eyes darting over each other, playing the old trick of pretending not to look. My head was reeling as I tried to make sense of it. His hand took mine and squeezed it gently. Neither of us said anything for almost a full minute, until I heard footsteps from down the hall.

"Are you dating her?" I asked, under my breath. I had to know. Forget the implications of the fact that I had just kissed my headmaster in a fiery passion that would have burned the school down—if his girlfriend was coming back as well, I might as well slit my wrists now.

"No." He laughed at the silliness of my question, and I felt he wasn't lying. "Porsche and I have a different story but romance doesn't have any part in it."

"Oh," I replied, looking away, as she returned to the room, first aid kit in hand.

"You're probably going to have to see a doctor, Amy," she said, crouching to my level. "But let's see if we can get the biggest shard out, hmm?"

"Uh huh." I extended my arm, glancing back at Liam. Our conversation ended abruptly, and I felt like a piece of me was unfinished.

Pulling a pair of tweezers from the first aid kit, she squinted in the light, examining the glass before clamping down on it. I braced myself, closing my eyes. The sun was almost gone now, setting fast, and I could practically see the last rays of light disappearing from behind my eyelids. I took a deep breath as I felt her brace my arm, and then she pulled.

It didn't hurt as much as I thought it would. When you grow up with IVs, needles and endless amounts of drugs and tests, you don't grow up squeamish. From behind me, however, I heard Liam grunt.

"Get out," Porsche said to him, quickly slapping some gauze on my wound, which had begun to ooze blood. I couldn't turn around, she had me gripped tightly, but I could hear him stand up. "Before you cause any more damage. You need to go. I already called Peter."

Peter was his grandfather, the old headmaster of the school. I could only assume he was being sent home on the infamous walk of shame. I smiled slightly to myself. Even Liam, the God of acting, was human.

"Maybe we could talk in the morning? I have … questions," I said, and Liam paused in the doorway, turning back to me. He was growing increasingly pale and I wondered if blood made him squeamish. But still, he gave me a devilish grin.

"Sure," he said, and then he was gone. Porsche rolled her eyes, wrapping my arm in gauze before checking my other wounds.

"Come on. We should get you to the school nurse."

"Right." I stood, shakily, taking her arm. "Is Liam going to be alright?"

She looked surprised as she helped me toward the door.

"He'll be fine, Amy," she said, although she didn't sound like she believed herself. "He always is."

CHAPTER 10: AMY

The next morning, I was up at the crack of dawn, my head still spinning from what had happened last night. I hadn't slept well at all, and part of that was due to the thin walls in the dorms. I knew I had it luckier than some of the students who had moved across the world to be here, some of them so young. I heard what I assumed was crying or moaning through the walls. And at first, my heart broke for whichever poor girl was so heartbroken that she was sobbing into her pillow.

By 3am, however, I had little pity for it, having been woken up twice. I actually fell asleep with my fingers in my ears, and they rang with exhaustion as I walked down the halls.

As soon as I knew Liam would be in his office I briskly walked down the hallways, trying not to draw attention to myself. In the hours since dawn, I had painstakingly done my makeup and paid more attention to my hair than I normally did. I put on the one pair of high heels I owned, trying not to pitch forward when I walked.

The hallways were mostly empty. The school officially opened at 8am but classes didn't start until 9am, and so I passed very few students.

Liam's door was closed, but I could see him through the shadowy glass window. Taking a deep breath and checking my reflection once more, I knocked twice.

"Yes?" his reply was brisk and curt through the door.

"It's Amy," I said, my voice shaking.

There was a silence and a shuffling of papers. Suddenly, the door opened. Liam stood there, looking crisp and sharp in the morning light; his shirt rolled up to his elbows and his pants perfectly pressed. The smell of a woodsy cologne drifted from his neck, and when he moved his arm to usher me in, I saw the ripple of lean muscle.

Once I was inside, Liam closed the door behind me and sat on the edge of the desk, watching me intently.

"How um…" I gulped. "How are you?"

"I'm fine," he said, his eyes never leaving mine. "How are you?"

"Also fine." I blushed, looking down at my shoes. For a moment, neither of us said anything, and then we both spoke at once.

"About last night…"

"Amy, last night…"

We both stopped, and laughed, awkwardly, nervously.

Finally, he spoke again, "Amy, last night was a mistake."

"Right," I swallowed the lump in my throat and tried to ignore the feeling of my stomach hitting the floor. "It was late, I was…clumsy and you were…not yourself and….I mean, of course, it was a mistake, this is something that can't happen, but don't worry, I won't tell anyone." I rose quickly. I just wanted to get out of there as soon as possible.

"Amy, Amy, Amy." He waved his hand with a small smile, motioning for me to sit back down. "Last night was a mistake because you didn't deserve to be treated that way. You're a young woman, a respectable young woman, and I should have approached you with respect … asked to court you, rather than act like a drunken lout."

My jaw fell open as I watched him pace the room slowly. He turned back to look at me, his eyes wide and full of question.

"So may I?"

I met his eyes, surprised.

"May you … what?"

"May I court you?" he asked. I almost fell off my chair.

"Uh…" came out of my throat, as he advanced and reached for my hand.

"Since the first time I saw you in the audition, you have captivated me for reasons I can't explain. Your talent, your grace, your beauty…" He was now just an inch away from my face, his warm breath making me blush. I had never felt anything like this before. My sexuality had always been something I pushed away. After all, when you grow up with HIV, you aren't exactly going to be having one night stands if you are any kind of decent person.

"Can we?" I asked, meaning a million different things. Up close, he was even more gorgeous; his eyes glinting in the soft sunlight; his hair perfectly styled; his skin glowing with passion. He shrugged, with a small smile.

"I make the rules around here," he said, leaning back to sit on the desk. "And I don't see why not. As long as you don't publicly announce it."

"I guess I'll cancel the National Press conference at 9 then," I said. A grin spread across my face and he kissed my hand with a good-natured growl.

"I've never done this before, Amy," he said, reading my mind. "It's not like with every new wave of students I find myself a hot date."

"I've never had a hot date...or a date..." I looked away, embarrassed.

He smiled, gently, brushing hair back from my forehead. "Well, then this will be a first time for both of us, won't it?" I nodded. "Although...Amy, we should lay down some ground rules."

"Like what?" I asked, hesitant to hear the answer. My heart was beating a million miles a minute at the sheer excitement of the situation. Liam thought for a moment before responding. More than anything, I wanted him to kiss me again, to take me in his arms. It was hard to focus, staring at his beauty and knowing now that I could have it if I wanted.

"We have to be careful where we are seen. Of course, there are things we won't be able to avoid. Like the fact that I can't take my eyes off of you in class." The statement made me blush, and I looked down. "But we must be careful about chatting too much in the hallways, or before or after class." I nodded, agreeing to this. "Also, we must be careful where we are seen. I know a way to your dorm...If you wanted to have dinner there, or perhaps my office...No one will question a new student wanting to spend extra hours catching up."

"But maybe we should do things off campus?" I suggested, getting into the spirit of things.

"Far off campus." He nodded, agreeing. "I have a car, there's a place a few towns over. But my celebrity status doesn't allow for much privacy, so we won't be able to stroll down the streets hand in hand."

"I think I can manage that," I said, with a nod, although part of me had forgotten he was a celebrity. Since I had gotten to know him, he was just Liam, the headmaster, my teacher, and now, my boyfriend. He grinned.

"Good," he said, standing up. "Shall I see you tonight then? You have a lot to catch up on. But perhaps we also have a lot to catch up on. I would like to know everything about you, Amy. Your hopes, your dreams, your aspirations. What you want from the world and from life."

"I …" I paused, trying to think of answers to those questions. When none came, I leaned in and kissed him. The kiss was different from last night. Last night was frantic, passionate and fiery. Today was soft and tender. We savored each moment and made sure every touch was well worth the wait. The effect was the same, and when we finally broke apart, I was panting again. He placed his hands on my waist, gripping me tightly.

"And I would like to know about you," I whispered, looking up to meet his eyes. Already, as if by magic, I could see a different person from the celebrity the whole world thought that they knew.

And so this was how the next few weeks panned out. Secret meetings, early morning rendezvous, empty classrooms and dark hallways. But it wasn't all passion and fire. One morning, I opened my door to check for the daily school paper that was left outside all the dorm rooms. Instead, I found a small item, wrapped in the daily paper.

Curious, I picked it up, looking up and down the hallways. However, there was no one there. Opening the package, a smile spread over my face. It was a tiny plastic Oscar with my name sharpied onto it. I rolled my eyes, laughing a bit as I turned it over in my hand. On the bottom, a sharpied heart was drawn. To my right, I heard a noise and looked up.

"Creative," I said, as Liam approached out of nowhere as usual. He smiled, looking around to double check that the hallways were empty. And then he kissed the top of my head, leading me into my dorm room.

"I thought you would appreciate that," he said, bending in for a deeper kiss.

I sighed happily, putting my arms around him. He smelled good, like wood smoke and whisky, something I couldn't describe but was instantly addicted to. His tongue explored my mouth and the intense passion in the early morning caused me to stumble. Before I knew it, we were pressed against a wall, my breath coming in gasps. With a devilish smile, he pulled back. "Good morning."

"Good morning," I said, sitting on my bed. He sat beside me, pulling open the brown bag he had been holding. From inside it wafted breakfast smells and he produced blueberry muffins. "Did you harass my father as soon as he got in the door? Only he makes these."

"I did. Perks of being headmaster," he replied, settling back against my headboard and taking a bite. He closed his eyes, and I watched his face for a moment.

"You look tired," I said, and he opened his eyes.

"Mmm. Rough night."

"Doing what?" I asked, and Liam shrugged.

"Wild partying, obviously," he said, although his tone was sarcastic. I could tell he didn't want me to pry so I didn't. I moved up beside him, biting into the familiar taste.

"Yeah, me too," I replied and he laughed. "Are you alright, though?"

"Fine now that I'm sitting beside you." He gave me a lazy smile, leaning his head against mine. "There used to be a time when a night of...that was all that would satisfy me. But now, I look forward to breakfast with you a lot more."

"What do you mean?" I asked, and he shrugged, taking my hand and squeezing it.

"You're all that I need right now," he replied, and I felt like nothing else mattered in the world but me at that moment.

"Do you believe in love?" I blurted out, and Liam turned to me, sharply. "Hypothetically, of course. In general. I'm not going all serious on you."

"I don't know," he said. "I don't. I haven't…before. You?"

"I think there are many cases of love in the world," I said. "But…I don't think love is true until it's returned. So you can be in love…but not until the other person returns it does it become real."

"And you've seen this?" he asked, fixated on my eyes. I didn't want to move as I was locked in his gaze.

"Not seen, not really. But heard about it. My parents … everyone talked about them. And my dad still talks about my mom like she's around. Not in a creepy way. She was the love of his life. She still is. And…" I traced a pattern on my bedspread, looking away. "Romeo loved Juliette, but it wasn't true love until she started paying attention. So you can be in love … but not true love?" I shrugged, embarrassed by my girly outpour of feelings. But Liam just took my chin, making me look at him again.

"That was beautiful, Amy. And probably right." He kissed the top of my head, and then wrapped his arms around me, pulling me tight. I shifted so I was on top of him, and he grinned like I had just given him an award. Compared to his body, I was small and thin, and I found a way to fit perfectly on top of him. When I was with him, I tried to forget all the things we couldn't do, and instead focused on all the things we could do. The sandwiches quickly forgotten, our kisses led to wandering hands, up and down each other's bodies.

86

Other times, it wasn't so serious. I remember walking into the theater early one morning, for Beauty and the Beast rehearsal, when I heard someone whisper my name. I spun around, but there was no one there.

Amy, came the voice again and I looked up. My heart was thudding with fear but again there was nothing.

"Hello?" I called, slowly walking toward the stage.

AMMMY. The voice got a little louder and seemed to be coming from all around me. I took a deep breath, climbing onto the stage. Up there, I felt like I could see everything and I was safe.

"Who's there? Who is this? Whoever it is, this isn't funny."

"Amy, you are destined for the stage."

The voice was echoing and bouncing off the walls. It was a man; that was all I could identify. Alone in the theater, I don't think I had ever been so scared. I put my hands at my sides, as if any amount of foreign space would open me for danger.

"How do you know?" I asked, looking up into the skylights.

"Because I'm watching," came the echo and I buried my head in my hands. Stories of Phantom of the Opera that we read in class last week, along with real theater ghost stories, came flooding back to my mind.

"And also..." the voice echoed, coming from all around me. "You are destined to not do your homework tonight."

I froze, pulling my hands away. A light came on in the projector booth and Liam popped his head out.

"...because we're having dinner."

"I HATE YOU!" I screamed at him, half laughing. Liam leaned against the balcony railing with a seductive smile on his face.

"So what do you think of our new sound system? It's all for the show."

"Argh, you." I tried to compose myself, but it was impossible with Liam looking down at me like that. "Come down here so I can punish you."

"I like the sound of that." He grinned, moving down the stairs. I stalked toward him, but he caught me in his arms, causing a giggle to escape from my lips. "So tell me how you are going to punish me."

"I'm not. Going. To. Kiss. You. All. Day." It was hard to get it out inbetween his onslaught of kisses, but I finally managed. "I swear it."

"Then I shall turn to dead at nightfall, my love," he said, giving me an old-fashioned bow. I rolled my eyes, heading back to the stage.

"Come on, Liam, let's rehearse."

There was one night however, that would stick in my mind forever.

We had a half day at school one Friday and Liam and I had long since agreed to spend the rest of the day together. However, it wasn't until nearly three o'clock that he knocked on my door.

I opened the door quickly, and he practically threw himself in. We had to be careful not to let anyone see him entering my dorm room too frequently. Already, questions were arising and the girls knew I was the "Teacher's Pet."

"Hey," I said, reaching to take his coat. Today, he wore dark jeans and a blue shirt, slightly open at the neck. He was absolutely perfect and I felt a bit bad that all I had on were my jeans and a tee-shirt. "Meetings run late?"

"There's a problem with Beauty and the Beast," he said, rolling his eyes as he went to sit on my bed. "Half of the committee feels that the publicity of me playing the lead wouldn't be worth depriving a student of the role."

"What?" I turned, stunned. "But you have to be Beast. I'm Beauty."

"I know." He wiggled his eyebrows at me, which made me laugh. "But perhaps they're right. I could at least cast someone for the role and have them play it most of the time. The one performance I do will be a special one for the press. And to teach this school how to act." He threw himself backward dramatically, lying on my bed. I came to sit beside him, folding my legs beneath me. This was often a complaint of Liam—that most of the school was only in it for the fame and glory.

"Can I act?" I asked, even though I already knew his answer. He turned his head toward me; a smile playing off his lips.

"Amy, when you act I forget that anything else exists but the world you are creating. Somehow, untrained, you understand more than the students who've had twelve years here. You're a diamond in the rough … an oasis in the desert. You're a…" We were interrupted by his stomach growling. I laughed.

"I'm a good girlfriend who feeds you good food, and that's the only reason you're here," I said, and he leaned on his elbows.

"That's part of it."

I had prepared oatmeal cookies last night when I went home to visit my father, and I brought out a plate of them now, placing them between us on the bed.

"How long can you stay?" I asked, and he stifled a yawn.

"A few hours of quality time, at least. I was wondering if you had given any thought to the dance class that was added to the semester."

I shrugged. "Only if it starts at a kindergarten level. I'm not a dancer. Who's teaching it?"

"A dance teacher from Russia," he said. "And a few guest instructors, like Porsche, when I can get them."

"Forget that then," I said, rolling my eyes. "I'll look like an elephant in a tutu."

"But a very cute one," he said, poking at the cookies.

"How did you meet Porsche?" I asked, and he cocked his head.

"Why?"

"Just curious," I said, with a casual shrug.

He took my hand, squeezing it. "Amy, I told you, there's absolutely nothing to be jealous of."

"I know," I replied, looking out the window as a kite flew by. "I just...want to know. Since she's your closest friend, right?"

"Right." He thought for a moment, and then shrugged. "We met at a party years ago. She was the life of the party, and I fell into her. Literally tripped. She's a fun girl and there are things about us that click, like the fact that we're both performers. But really, Amy, it's not like that." He pulled me closer, laying a light kiss on my lips.

I nodded, savoring the kiss. There was something about Liam's eyes that told me there was more to the story but I didn't question it.

When I had told Sarah the whole story, she had of course questioned everything; his friendship with Porsche, the legality of the fact that he was my teacher, the age gap, everything. Sometimes I think she wanted me to film every aspect of my life and play it back for her.

Of course, I had not told my father. I couldn't imagine how severe his reaction would be. Dad also wanted an account of my actions every moment of the day, and I knew he was starting to notice the huge gaps of time that went un-talked about—the times I snuck away to spend with Liam.

I wasn't sure if any of the other students or faculty members had noticed either. I mean, before this, the girls knew I was Liam's favorite, and I suffered for it. But nothing had changed in that respect, so perhaps they hadn't noticed. As for the faculty, I was quite sure they'd bring it to his attention and not mine but he hadn't said anything to me about needing to be more careful. The only one who I thought might be in on the secret was his secretary, who kept her face deliberately blank as I came and left his office day after day.

She must have heard the goings-on; who couldn't? Liam and I could entertain each other perfectly for days just cracking jokes, or rehearsing. But more often than not, when we had private time, that's not what we were doing. I was sitting in his lap, my legs wrapped around him, as we made out; or running my hands along his chest as we sank to the floor. He was going to drive me crazy before the year was up, I could tell.

And although it was wonderful, it was the times we sat and talked that I enjoyed the most.

Taking the remote, I turned on the television and flipped through the channels.

"What are we watching?" asked Liam, his mouth full of cookies.

"We...are...watching...this," I finally landed on *Shakespeare in Love*, the opening credits just rolling. He shrugged and I settled back into his arms, munching on a cookie myself. As the movie began to play, I closed my eyes, feeling warm, comfortable and safe against Liam. He gave me a squeeze, wrapping his strong arms around me and we settled further into the pillows. Soon the cookie tray was empty. We put it aside and sprawled out on the bed. Cuddling close to him as the movie went on, I fell asleep.

My cell phone ringing woke me up with a jolt. The room was a lot darker than the last time my eyes were open and the TV was now playing an endless infomercial. I leapt up to grab it.

"Hello?" I asked, frantic and still groggy with sleep.

"Can I speak to Amy?" said a female voice. I recognized the drone of a call center in the background and rolled my eyes.

"No, she's out right now," I said and hung up, turning back to Liam who sat up abruptly, also startled by the noise.

"What time is it?" he asked, running a hand over his face.

"Uh...8" I said, and he jumped up immediately. "Everything ok? Liam?" I grabbed his arm as he shot past me, taking his coat from the hanger. "Are you ok? You look a bit pale."

"I'm fine, but I have to go," he said, not looking at me. He laid a quick kiss on my cheek and hurried toward the door, not even pausing for a cautious minute to make sure the hall was empty. "I'll see you tomorrow, Amy," he said, and practically slammed the door behind him. I stood in the middle of the floor confused, and wondered how a telemarketer cell phone call had possibly offended him.

Mind you, we had never fallen asleep together before. While comfortable for me, I realized it may have made him feel uncomfortable—especially this early on. With a shrug, I switched off the TV and pulled my hair into a bun. I had homework to finish anyway.

Around 10pm, I closed my books, sighing. I was well into the work I needed to do, and I could have kept going, had it not been for that noise again. Every evening, around this time, I could hear someone crying as if their soul was breaking through the walls. At first I assumed it was a homesick student, or maybe a student who had had a bad day—something that would be temporary and go away. But this was continuous as if they were on a timer. Every night at dark, it sounded like someone was being tortured.

I checked my phone for messages; something to distract me. It seemed the whole world was busy tonight, and there was still no word from Liam. I stood up to grab a sweater, checked my appearance in the mirror briefly and went out the door.

The hallways were quiet and empty. I knew the sound was always coming from my left side, and so I ventured that way, careful to make sure my steps were quiet. Just a little way down, to my left, was a hallway that led to a fire escape. No one ever went down there. The light was constantly broken and the door was always locked. But, glancing back to my room, I realized it would make sense if the sound was coming from there.

I walked down the hallway, using my phone as a flashlight as I neared the end of it. Biting my lip, I casually tried the door. To my surprise, it was open this time.

I looked up quickly to make sure I wasn't about to set off a trip wire and a fire alarm. One thing I had learned from sneaking around the school in my younger days was what the alarm system looked like. However, this door had no wiring, just the sign, and I wondered if it was simply a decoy.

There was a set of stairs behind the door, again badly lit. Using my phone, I could see that there was dust everywhere, aside from the middle, where there were footprints. Someone had been here, and recently as well.

Taking a deep breath to steel myself, I started down the steps, making sure my foot was firmly on one step before I went to the next one. I was definitely moving in the right direction; the noise was getting louder.

At the bottom of the steps was a huge steel door that looked like it was left over from another century. The moaning was coming from in there and the door was slightly ajar. Even though I knew I shouldn't, I couldn't resist. Creeping forward, I peered through the crack.

What I saw was a sight I would never forget.

Liam was chained to the wall, with cuffs around his wrists that he was trying to break free of. But it was his face that would stick in my mind forever. He was pale as a corpse and his teeth were nearly poking out of his mouth due to their length and sharpness. His eyes were black and his muscles seemed more defined. He didn't look like the Liam I knew at all, more like a dark shadow of himself. What softened me was that he seemed to be in pain.

94

"Liam?" I squeaked, my voice barely above a whisper. His head snapped up and he snarled at me, causing me to jump back.

"Amy," he said. His voice was devoid of emotion. I turned, but he reached out, confined by the chains. "Wait, Amy….don't go. It was foolish to think I could hide this forever."

"Hide WHAT?" I asked, unable to take my eyes off what he had become. Liam laughed, although there was no humor in his tone.

"What do you think?" he asked. "Look at me. Look at me and tell me what do you think?"

"Are you…sick?" I asked, taking a step forward again. "Is there something wrong? Because I can deal with being sick, Liam, obviously."

"And part of the reason I can deal with you is that you are," he said, looking straight into my eyes. "Your blood does not smell as tempting as a normal person's would. Your illness is my blessing."

I stared at him, shocked.

"How could you say that?" I asked. "How could you say that…?"

"Amy." He shook his head, and then groaned again. Out of sympathy, I took another step forward, even though I was trembling with fear. "You don't have to be afraid. These chains have held me almost every night for three years. They'll hold now. And even if they don't…I won't hurt you, Amy. Ever."

Suddenly, it dawned on me. All the facts were swimming in my head. Stunned, I felt dizzy, and sat on the ground, a few feet from Liam. I held my head, trying to make sense of the clues he was giving me.

"What are you, Liam?" I asked, finally.

"What do you think?" he asked, baring his fangs at me. The word burned on my tongue, but I didn't want to say it. I felt like I was going to pass out.

"Is this a joke?"

"Yes, Amy, it's a joke. An elaborate hoax, and every night I visit the hair and makeup department in the hopes of tricking you." He turned his face toward mine, and I saw the scars of tears.

"Why are you crying?" I asked, sympathy overtaking me. He winced.

"Because it hurts."

"Why?" I was here now, and whether I believed him or not, I wanted to hear his answer.

"Legend has taught you to believe that vampires are forever in their demonic form, day and night, and can't walk in the sun," he said, leaning against the wall. "But the truth is, the reason you don't see vampires in the sunlight is because we are human during the day. And every night, as darkness takes the city, we die and change. It's a painful process and we crave blood every second of the night. And then, as the sun rises, our hearts start to beat again, our demonic form recedes, and we change back."

"That night. We first kissed," I spoke in a voice I felt was not my own. "I saw...you looked different."

"Yes. I shouldn't have stayed that long," he said, shaking his head. "But then, we didn't expect you."

"We," I repeated. "Porsche knows?"

He laughed at that.

"Yes, she knows. And unlike Peter, who thinks I should stay in every night and fight it, Porsche encourages me to be who I am. If I go out at night, it's always with her."

"Peter locks you up here?" I said, aghast and he nodded.

"Don't look so surprised, Amy, it's my choice. As much as I crave blood, I don't really want to spend every night on a killing spree."

"Do you?" I asked, watching him. "Do you kill?"

"Sometimes," he said, although he seemed truly sorry for it. "As the popular stories go, we can survive on animal blood, but it's not always very fun."

I fell silent. I couldn't deny what he was saying. There was too much evidence in front of me.

"Is that why you hang out with Porsche? Her blood is infected?"

"And she's fun>" He gave me a cheeky grin. "But nothing compares to you."

"And that's why you chose me," I said. "At the audition."

This time, his face darkened, and he shook his head.

"No, Amy. I chose you because you truly were the best. Something drew me to you, and I didn't know what it was. But you weren't the only girl who tried out who had a chronic illness. You weren't the first and you won't be the last. It was your raw talent that got you chosen ... that's all."

I took a deep breath, drawing my knees up to my chest.

"Do you sleep?" I asked, unable to rein in my curiosity. He nodded.

"I do. You saw me do it. Just not regularly. We don't need as much sleep as humans, so usually, a quick nap from dawn to the start of school does me fine, and perhaps a power nap during the day. Nothing to throw my schedule off." He shrugged.

"So it hurts?" I asked, and he nodded.

"I die. And then, just when I get used to it, I live again."

A silence came over us. I placed my head on my knees, trying to make sense of everything that had happened. My head was spinning. It seemed unreal and yet I couldn't deny what was staring me in the face.

"Are you immortal, Liam?" I asked, and he nodded, watching my face. I knew I couldn't hide the reaction that came over it. Looking immortality in the face, and challenging it with my own weak body; my own clear mortality, made my chest ache. Tears sprung to my eyes, and although I turned away, I knew that Liam saw them.

"It's not as good as it's cracked up to be," he said.

"How long have you been this way?" I asked, visions running through my head of Liam fighting in the Civil War and living like a cave man.

"Three years," he replied. "That's why I left Hollywood. But I couldn't leave acting altogether, I just couldn't. The years I spent in Hollywood had already made me push people away, except for superficial friendships, so it wasn't hard to continue that way. Peter was...the only one I remained close to and the only one I kept by my side through all this. He's very understanding...of all of it. Of this, the old ways, the curse."

I cocked my head.

"The curse?" I asked, and Liam shook his head at me.

"A story for another time, Amy."

We fell into silence for a moment, and then I asked him the question that had been playing in my mind the whole time.

"How the hell did this happen to you?"

He watched me silently for a few minutes. It was hard to look at his face but I held my gaze.

"Would you like to know?"

I nodded, and he took a deep breath.

"Then perhaps you should make yourself more comfortable, because it's a long story."

CHAPTER 11: LIAM

The paparazzi were getting worse every day and veterans told me it was just the beginning. I was starting to associate outdoors with danger and indoors with safety. Lately, so much of my vision had been tunnel; focus on the door to the club; the store; the studio; and get to it. It wasn't really acceptable for male actors, especially at my age, to have bodyguards. So I was on my own. I weaved through the crowd, keeping my head down and my mouth shut as I tumbled through the door to the club.

The atmosphere inside was smoky. The club was packed to the rafters even though the sun was just setting. Every hour was Happy Hour in Hollywood. All I wanted was a stiff drink, perhaps an illicit cigarette, and to get lost in the crowd.

"Triple vodka on the rocks," I half screamed, half signed to the barman, who nodded. Bar language was different than regular language and I had a theory that only actors succeeded at it because of their extensive facial expressions and powerful lungs.

My drink arrived swiftly in a tall water glass that tempted me just to take a few swift chugs and send it back. Instead I gripped it and turned around to look for an empty table. There weren't any actual seats—just the tall bar tables where people half stood and half danced the night away.

Squinting into a dark corner, there was a table with only one person standing there, alone. Getting closer, I was stunned. And that didn't usually happen in the land of Hollywood beauty. Tall and thin; she was dressed all in black, with a sheet of dark hair falling down her back. Her skin was as pale as snow and her eyes were rimmed with kohl. She didn't seem to be performing the usual charade of a single person in a club. Instead, she truly seemed to be absorbed in her own world, quite content in her loneliness.

"LIAM!" I turned around, surprised to find Kaitlin and William crunched along a table full of familiar faces. They were mostly actors, but some were behind the camera; a producer and a makeup artist. "Come here! Scrunch over everyone, make room for Liam!"

"Uh..." I paused a moment, looking at the smiling faces that welcomed me. I suppose if I wanted to be alone I shouldn't have come out to a club...yet, from behind me, I could feel the mystery woman. I could feel her eyes burning through me. I glanced over my shoulder, and found, to my surprise, that she was looking right at me. "Perhaps in a bit...I'm meeting someone."

Everyone laughed and nodded knowingly. Apparently my reputation for womanizing was well known, as it should be. But this...this felt different. This woman, even as I approached her, was a divine creature. There wasn't one ounce of imperfection that I could see on her; not one wrinkle or blemish. She did not react as I neared her as most people did these days. Instead, a slow smile spread across her face.

"Bonjour," she said, slowly.

"Hello," I replied, pointing to the empty spot at the table. God, she was beautiful. "Can I ...stand here?" When exactly did I turn into a quivering child? There was something about her that made me unable to take my eyes off her.

"Of course." When she spoke, she had a thick French accent that added to her exoticness.

"I'm Liam." I extended my hand and she shook it. Her fingers were thin and her nails were perfectly manicured. What surprised me was the coolness of her skin, even in the sweaty club.

"Selene," she drawled, her eyes giving me the once over that I had given other women many times over the past few years.

"And what do you do?" I asked her. With looks like this, I was certain she was in the industry.

"I'm an ... ambassador," she said smoothly, and I assumed by her French accent that she meant between France and here. I was impressed. I took a sip of my drink and watched how she moved ever so slightly to the music. "And you?"

I raised an eyebrow. There wasn't anyone in this town who didn't know who I was. Either she was lying or she really had just arrived.

"I'm an actor." Already the few sips of the drink were warming me. I felt more relaxed and utterly entranced, watching her every movement.

"Ah...acting. Believe in untrue circumstances," she said, with a small smile. "And do you believe things that used to be untrue, Liam?"

"Of course." I nodded, and she leaned in, those exotic eyes glinting in the light.

"I hope I can make you believe a few, tonight."

"I hope you can," I replied with a smirk, my hand inching across the table to take hers again.

"Your place or mine?"

"Yours," she replied, drawing closer to me. She didn't have a bag or purse to pick up and I instantly liked that about her. Women could be so complicated, I wanted something simple. "It'd be better if you were to wake up there."

"All right then." I wrapped my arm around her waist, which was small and lean but compact with muscle. As she leaned in, her lips teasing the soft flesh behind my ear, I had to control the urge to

grab her and take her right there. But before we got to the door, I stopped her. "Listen...I'm rather well-known here. So it's likely there'll be a cloud of paparazzi outside."

"They'll forget one night," she said huskily in my ear. "But you won't."

Sure enough, the cameras began flashing as soon as we exited. I put my arm around her neck, pulling her head down a bit to protect her identity. She didn't seem to mind or even notice as her hand slipped under my shirt, indicating things to come. I chalked up the oddness in her speech to the fact that English was clearly her second language. She spoke slowly, and deliberately, looking at me for what I assumed was an indication that I understood her words. Still, there was no lack of confidence that usually came with speaking a second language ... no pause of uncertainty or flicker of embarrassment. It was almost as if she was trying to imply a double meaning with everything she said. But whatever that meaning was, I was too lost in her eyes to get it.

I felt drunk on the limo ride back, my senses swimming. It didn't make any sense, I had left my drink half untouched. But something about this woman, her accent in the setting sun, turned me into a stumbling teenager about to get his first kiss. We barely made it up to my apartment before the clothes began to come off.

I locked the door and pushed her down on the bed. She ran her hands over my body as I struggled to unbutton her dress. I stood up as the sunlight disappeared, causing her to moan.

"Just wait," I said, heading toward the light switch. "You're the most stunning creature I have ever seen and I want to see every inch of you."

I flicked the light switch on, and my heart almost stopped there and then.

"Creature is right," she said, with a sneer, showing fangs. She was what I brought home, yet extremely different. Paler than before, with dark circles around her eyes, her mouth had stretched as fangs appeared. And those beautiful eyes were now black as night.

I stumbled back against the wall, shocked. I felt my breath coming in gasps as I tried to make sense of what I saw in front of me. How much, exactly, had I had to drink?

"What the…" I said, as she got up, approaching me with such slow deliberate movements that I knew I was finished. "What are you?"

"Well, Liam, I'm what you are," she replied. "Or…what you will be. You'll be our ambassador now, and you can never hide. So you'll keep us safe."

"What are you talking about?" I gasped, reaching behind me. Even though I knew it was there, my hand was trembling so badly I couldn't open the door knob. "What are you?"

"I'm a vampire, Liam. And so are you."

I put my hands up to block her from coming at me, but she was impossibly strong and fast.

"Liam, Liam," she said, as she held my hands in a death grip, almost crushing my bones. "Don't look so afraid. You were chosen from thousands. With your fame, you will protect our identity forever; we know you'll do anything to make sure our secret is safe. Because now our secret is also yours."

The last thing I remembered was the instant pain of her fangs sinking into my neck; the slow agony as her poison filled my blood. I felt my head hit the ground, and then, blessed darkness.

xxxxxxxxxxxxxxxxxxxxxxxxxxxxxxxxxxxxxxxxx

When I awoke, it was still dark. My head was pounding, my mouth was dry, and I felt like I was coming off a nine day bender. I groaned, dragging myself upward from my spot on the floor, not entirely sure how I got there.

My stomach felt like it was made of acid and I couldn't decide if I was ravenously hungry or about to be sick. To be safe, I made my way to my bathroom, my legs unsteady as I leaned against the wall. I was trying to make sense of what had happened; trying to remember.

When I turned on the light, however, it all came back.

A scream came out of my throat, almost animalistic as I saw myself in the mirror. Like her, I was pale as a ghost, my teeth long and sharp, and my eyes dark as night. I looked again, and again, each time unbelieving.

"No. It can't be real. It can't be real," I said. In my pocket, my phone beeped, and I reached for it instinctively. My horror was not at the 69 missed calls, 200 emails and 47 text messages that flashed on the screen. My horror was the date above it. I had lost nearly three days.

Frantically, I opened my contact book scrolling through it. I wanted comfort. I wanted safety. I wanted someone to explain what was happening to me. But as I went through the names, I realized there was no one I could trust who would believe such a wild tale. I didn't even fully believe it myself. This couldn't be real. It had to be a joke, a drug laced trip. Perhaps I had drunk more than I should. Perhaps I hit my head and my mind was making up stories.

But nothing explained my appearance in the mirror or the fact that I craved thick liquid to slurp; warm and salty. I craved blood.

I had to find her. I had to figure out what was happening.

I grabbed a pair of sunglasses and a ball cap—the standard garb of celebrities trying to hide. My clothes felt disgusting but I allowed myself no time to change.

I hit the pavement quickly; a light drizzle of rain meant it was mostly empty. My energy burned inside me, and I felt I could walk the five miles to the club; my last link to her.

Until I smelled him.

There was a man coming toward me, his clothes ripped and his left hand gripped over his right. He was walking quickly, his jaw set in what I guessed must be pain. I could smell the blood coming from the wound on his hand, and I couldn't help but stop.

"You ok, man?" I asked, clenching my fists. All I could think about was the warm liquid that was pouring from his veins.

"I just got mugged!" he exclaimed. "Bastard knifed me and took my wallet and phone. Dude, do you have a cell phone? Please, I need to call the police."

"Yeah, yeah, sure," I said, reaching into my pocket and handing it to him.

"Thanks, dude," he said, and removed his hand from his wound to take the phone and dial. There were emails with subject lines that revealed my name, and he must have seen it. However, the surprise on his face was not my concern. "Hey, are you..."

I couldn't control my muscles, couldn't stop myself from launching forward at him, bearing my fangs and letting out an

106

animalistic growl. We crashed into the alley behind us, his screams echoing through the passageway. With anger I couldn't explain, I hit him, my hand connecting so hard with his face, it drew blood.

That was too much for me, and my body moved before my mind thought. I sunk my fangs into his neck, and once I started, I couldn't stop. It was like I was famished, and this man was a buffet. I drank until his body was dry.

Drawing back when there was no more blood, I began to shake again. His body lay drained in front of me, so obviously dead that I knew there was no point in calling 9-1-1. Tears began to fall down my face, coming in great gasps, and I couldn't hold back. I felt sadness and fear wash over me in ways I had never felt before. I was cold, the rain soaking through my clothes, and while the external pain of earlier had passed, the tightness in my chest was growing unbearable.

The man's hand still gripped my cell phone, and I reached out slowly, taking it. The battery was dying, although there was probably enough juice left for one call.

When I moved to Hollywood five years ago, I hadn't left my home on good terms. My family thought trying to be an actor was the stupidest move I could make. It was a pipedream full of bad morals and worse behavior, and if I left, I left without their blessing. Over the last five years, the angry phone calls from home became shorter, and then stopped coming. They hadn't changed their minds. They didn't approve, so contact was cut.

And as the glamorous shiny world of fast friends and faster lovers surrounded me, my friends back home eventually drifted out of my life as well. They weren't replaced. No, Hollywood wasn't a place of tight brotherhood where you shared things. You shared drinks, and women, and strip clubs. You flashed your money around as fast as you could, and bragged, but there wasn't any friendship.

I brought the phone to my ear, listening to it ring overseas. There was still one person who hadn't abandoned me; one person, who had told me to follow my dream and listened when I talked. One person who believed every word out of my mouth and gave me the best advice I could have ever received.

"Hello?" came a voice over the phone, gruff with age. That's when I lost it; the tears turning to sobs and hysterics. I couldn't talk. I couldn't breathe. I was acting like a child instead of a man. "Hello? Who's there? Liam?"

I took a deep breath, trying to steady myself for a few moments.

"Grandpa? I need your help. Can I come over?"

I heard a pause over the phone line, and a million questions catch in his throat. But he asked none of them.

"Of course, my boy. Tell me when your plane gets in."

xxxxxxxxxxxxxxxxxxxxxxxxxxxxxxxxxxxxxx

At first, Peter didn't believe me. Anyone who did right off the bat probably needed help themselves. But it only took one night, one night where he stayed in the room and watched the horrible transformation, to believe every word that tumbled out of my mouth from then on.

Peter took pity on me and allowed me to escape Hollywood; offering me a job as a teacher at the Academy for the rest of the term. I could still be immersed in acting, and yet stay out of Hollywood.

We found out that alcohol stunned the cravings, as it stunned most of your body's other senses. And, before we figured out that I needed to be tied up every night if I didn't want to kill anybody, I found Porsche.

I had stumbled upon a redneck high school party in the woods, a bunch of poor kids with beer kegs and bad wine. Drinking from one of them could easily be explained away as an accident. Kids will do stupid things and no one is ever sober enough to remember.

But just as I was about to make my move, Porsche, already 12 years into her dance training and on the brink of her own fame, grabbed me, her confidence enhanced by her popularity. She recognized me, of course, everyone still did, and she knew she wanted to land the superstar at the party. But when she touched me, everything disappeared. My cravings and fangs receded and my body began to warm up. She is one of the most powerful Shields to ever live, and she was unclaimed, living in solidarity as well.

Her identity and skill must also be kept a secret. While supernatural beings can use Shields to protect themselves or seek other supernatural beings out, Shields are also mortal and usually their powers intensify in illness, like Porsche. Once claimed by a supernatural being—a witch, a werewolf, a vampire—they usually don't survive past the first battle simply because their mortality stands out in a room full of immortals.

I didn't want to go to battle with her. What I wanted was a friend who could understand me and help guide me through this supernatural life. I didn't claim her, didn't take her to a witch to put a binding spell on us. There was no need for formalities. Our friendship began on common ground and remained strong on the understanding that we needed each other.

It was Porsche who told me how to survive as a vampire. Together, we figured out everything I needed to know. We figured out when the transformation started and stopped; we figured out that animal blood could do it, if need be. We managed to separate what we thought were myths about vampires from facts. We could walk in sunlight. We could breathe, eat, drink and sleep in sunlight. We are alive in the daytime, only cursed at night. At night, we are immortal creatures with no heart beat or pulse; just a thirst for blood. The legends were correct in the weapons of our death. Wooden stakes through the heart and fire were our bane. Decapitation also worked, although that was hard; with our veins hardening and our muscles turning partially to stone every night. Even minor good things, like having a horrid cold during the day and feeling fine at night, didn't cheer me up.

Selfishly wanting to keep her by my side; wanting someone to understand, I gave her the first scholarship that was mine to give so she could remain at the school and help me. Peter retired at the end of the term, giving me the position of headmaster. He was thinking of doing it anyway, and with my arrival and lack of ability to return, he saw the perfect opportunity. The role of headmaster suited me perfectly. I could teach the classes I wanted, put on the shows I loved, and I was important enough to blow everyone off at night. My reputation as an arrogant egotistic actor only came in handy, as people gave me the space I needed once the sun went down.

The reputation at the Academy only grew with my presence, and within six months, we were the biggest and the best. We could charge anything we wanted, and people would pay. Our productions became on par with Broadway and the West End. Even when Porsche left for the Russian National Ballet, visiting only occasionally, I thought I would be fine. I had settled into a life that made me happy. I could survive this. I figured out I needed to be locked away. I didn't want to cause a scene anymore; I didn't want to kill or leave bodies; or have any more attention. I could live on animals most nights and no one got hurt. Except me.

And that's when Selene started to show up again. She only came at night when I was locked away feeding on a rabbit or a squirrel. And she was even more irresistible than the first night I met her. By night, both in our demon form, she had power over me as my sire. It was like I was a puppet and she was my master. When she was here, I was under her spell and she owned every inch of me. She asked for the key to the chains and I told her where it was without hesitation. When she appeared, we would roam the streets with my mind under her influence and my hand locked in hers.

I would spend weeks in depression after she left; my human emotions coming strong when the sun rose. Covering up those deaths, deaths that I know I caused, was the hardest of all. Occasionally, I considered turning myself in and giving the families some peace. But I couldn't bring myself to do it ... not with the repercussions it would cause.

She chose me because of my power in Hollywood, my influence around the world, because she knew I would do anything to protect my image, and she was right. I knew how to cover up media stories and press releases. I knew how to spin a tale to make it seem innocent or accidental. Soon, whether I wanted to or not, it was me who was making phone calls, spinning tales, protecting vampires around the world whenever they did anything that could reveal what they really were. There was even a photo of me released one night, taken from God knows where, when I was in vampire form. It was an easy spin. I just claimed it was a makeup test for a new theater role, but it scared me. I became more of a recluse; throwing myself into the theater, pushing everyone but Peter and Porsche away. I increased security and never left the grounds. I protected the school and myself every way I could.

Eventually, Selene stopped showing up and I currently was 8 months without her presence—which scared me even more. Either she had grown tired of me, or she was biding her time, waiting for a moment, but it was unclear to me. But whatever the reason, she wasn't here and hadn't been for months.

xxxxxxxxxxxxxxxxxxxxxxxxxxxxxxxxxxxxxxxx

As I neared the end of my story, I felt my fangs begin to recede.

"What time is it, Amy?" I asked, jerking her out of the trance that she had settled into. It had broken my heart to not see a flicker of reaction on her face as she listened and I was becoming increasingly anxious to hear her thoughts. But like a good actress, she hid the emotions she did not want me to see.

"5 AM," she replied, glancing at her watch. Her voice was dead too, and it nearly killed me. I knew I was transforming back. I could already feel my breath coming stronger and the familiar stirring in my chest as my heart began to beat. "I'm tired," she said, unfolding herself and slowly rising. "It's been a long night."

"Amy," I called, when I finally couldn't take it anymore. She glanced at me, her eyes heavy with fatigue. "It doesn't change anything. Amy, there's a million things that we don't know about each other, and I would be happy to spend a lifetime telling you everything. But the thing you need to know right now is that I spent my whole life alone. I was a teenager in Hollywood and I made stupid mistakes, of course. I played the big roles in the movies, but I didn't for one second believe in star-crossed lovers. I didn't believe two people were meant to be together, or even could possibly want each other beside one night in the darkness. But then I met you, Amy, and I changed. My whole world fell upside down, even though I was not searching for it. I thought I wanted the darkness, and I found the light instead. I need you, Amy." I meant it, desperately trying to search her eyes for some flicker of hope. But I saw none. She shook her head, taking a few steps back.

112

"I need to get some sleep, Liam," she replied. "I have class in a few hours."

"You can ... not go to class?" I offered. "We can talk some more. Anything. Anything you want." The last thing I wanted was for her to back away and leave.

"No." She shook her head. "I don't want to talk some more. I don't ... I don't want to talk to you again."

"Amy!" I cried, feeling my heart crack.

"I can't do this, Liam," she said, and I could see the tears in her eyes. "I can't do this. I'm sorry. You're immortal...and I'm too mortal for this."

"That doesn't matter," I tried to argue. "Amy, please"

"No. Your heart is cursed, Liam; cursed and belonging to someone else. That much is clear." She was almost at the door now. I shook my head, wanting to cry out that none of this was true, but words escaped me. "Please leave me alone. Please just leave me alone."

And then she was gone, the door slamming behind her. I heard her footsteps run up the stairs, as if the devil was behind her. And I guess he was.

The sadness hit me like a rock. Tears pricked my eyes and I started having hysterics. I was so tired and hurt. Emotion was controlling me like Selene often did. I couldn't lose Amy. Not this way, not like this.

A million horrible thoughts poured into my mind, none of them logical. The only one that made sense was a fact: I was alone in this room, and in this world. Utterly and truly alone.

CHAPTER 12: AMY

I don't think I slept for two days straight. I went to the school nurse as soon as I escaped Liam. I needed an excuse to get out of class. Luckily, having infected blood is apparently a reason to get out of class anytime. The one obstacle that stood in my way, however, was my father.

"Please don't call him," I said to the nurse, as I got my coat, a note clutched in my hand. "I'll tell him myself. But really, I just need a day or two to rest. It's scarier to him if someone else calls him. If I can do it myself, it shows I'm ok. He's under a lot of stress right now."

She sighed and then put down the contact book she was flipping through.

"All right. You're old enough to make your own choices, Amy. But if things get worse you need to come to me right away."

"Of course." I nodded, zipping up my coat and then heading out of the office. Now, I was safe. Liam wouldn't come looking for me for days, I knew that, and an official record of an excuse from class meant no one else would either. As long as I still met my dad for lunch, he wouldn't suspect a thing.

I didn't want to do anything but shut myself in my room for days. Even though it was impossible to believe, I knew what Liam told me was true. There was no other explanation for what I had seen. The way his face had changed in the darkness and then changed again in the light; the fact that I never saw him after dark; the way he ran off as soon as the sun was setting. All the facts began to add up and I wondered why I didn't see it before.

I couldn't deal with this. I couldn't handle it. It was almost like, wordlessly, he was mocking me. My mortality loomed with every beat of my heart … with every beep of my watch to remind me to take my AZT. Without them, the disease would descend and I'd be dead in less than a few years. They kept my death at bay but reminded me that the Grim Reaper was constantly looming over me.

I spent a good part of the day angry at him. He didn't think it was something important to tell me when we first got involved? And still, even the fact that he had been cursed and made immortal didn't seem so bad to me. Liam didn't need to sleep. He was only a vampire at night. He had gone from one incredibly successful career to another without so much as lifting a finger. Everything had been handed to him. He had never known struggle or poverty, and yet he thought he had the right to complain about his troubles.

I paced the room, resisting the urge to throw something. How could I trust anything that came out of his mouth now? All those things he had promised me—parts, help, fame, schooling—I wondered if any of it was true. Or was I simply a relief for him; a potential snack that didn't tempt him?

How could I have been so stupid to even think I was talented? I smelled terrible to him and that's why he wanted me around. He would rather have me, for his own selfish reasons—to be able to kiss and touch and be around a warm human he didn't want to eat—than choose someone who actually deserved this scholarship and would be good for the school.

I wasn't about to give it up, of course. No, I decided that late on the second day as I sat on my bed, furiously typing away at my laptop. My disease had given me nothing but trouble, but for one miracle moment it had actually helped me. This was *my* dream and it didn't matter what the reason was for it happening. I mean, Hollywood was all about whom you knew, not what you could do. Everyone knew that. So if this was the reason I got here, so be it. Liam wasn't going to take it away from me.

Angrily, I slammed my laptop shut and got up. I stalked to my bedroom door to check the schedule I had taped there. I had rehearsal first thing in the morning and I decided I was going. He wasn't going to take away anything more from me. If my blood got me here, so be it, but my talent was going to keep me here. I was going to try as hard as I could because I knew another shot like this would never happen again. Even if I had to do it alone.

I picked up my phone and sent an email to my instructors, informing them I would be resuming classes in the morning. There were several messages from Sarah. I knew I had ignored her over the past two days. Two days was the longest we'd come without ever speaking. I couldn't do it any longer, even if I couldn't tell her exactly what was happening.

With a sigh, I glanced in the mirror, making sure I didn't look too upset with the world. And then, I pushed the video call button. She answered immediately.

"Amy, where the hell have you been? Are you ok? I was worried! What's going on, girl?"

"Nothing," I said, settling back on my bed with what I hoped was a bored sigh. This was probably my greatest acting challenge to date. And if I was going to keep being an actress, then I'd better get used to it. "I've just been really busy. Rehearsal and all. I'm tired, tell me about you!"

She grinned, sitting down on her own couch. "I went to this audition today…" As Sarah babbled on, I settled my head back against the pillows, listening. Normal life had to resume, or at least what was left of it. It had to or I wouldn't survive. It just had to resume without Liam.

CHAPTER 13: AMY

The next morning, my alarm pierced through the silence at 6am. It was the earliest I could manage to get up and still feel half decent. The dancers often got up at 5am, as they were used to having to go to rehearsals before and after normal schooling. Now that they were here, they used every waking moment to practice.

I knew, however, that I would be the first awake in the drama wing. My fellow actors were the ones who were rushing down the halls to class with less than a minute to spare, on a daily basis.

I turned on the shower, relying on the water to wake me up. Last night, I had printed a fresh copy of my script, and transferred notes from the mangled one. Three days ago, I would have still felt disappointed that Liam had gone through with his choice to have someone else play Beast for almost all the shows. Today, I was glad of it.

My new partner, Deon, was a senior student, and a great actor. He had been at the school since he was six, and he knew every trick. He was funny, and kind, and took time to explain to me some terms I had not yet grasped in class. We got along well in class, and I knew rehearsal was going to be fine.

Out of the shower, I dried my hair and applied a bit of makeup. It wasn't something I normally wore, but this was the new me; the me without Liam; the me who could make it on her own.

By 7am, I was walking down the halls of the dorms, toward the theater. I barely glanced at the hallway with the nearly invisible door where I had found Liam. I couldn't change the truth about him, but I could move on.

He hadn't tried to contact me at all in the past two days, nor had I messaged him. I guessed my dramatic exit had made it clear that I couldn't deal with this.

I did miss him, of course, although it was hard to admit it. I missed his arms around me, his sweet gentle kisses that came and went too fast when we snuck away to my room on lunch hour. I missed his guidance with my work, and rehearsing alone in my room without anyone to point out flaws was starting to send me in a panic.

But all that had to be behind me. Whatever issues Liam was working through weren't mine to deal with. How could I trust him ever again?

I hadn't expected to find anyone in the theater at 7am. I had checked online, and it wasn't booked by anybody. The rooms at school were open from 6.30am until midnight to all students to practice what they needed. Bigger rooms, like this theater, had to be booked in advance or used with the understanding that someone could book it at any time. I hadn't bothered, but I had figured no one else would be up this early. And I was right.

And so became my routine. Up early every morning, before the rest and into the theater just as the janitor unlocked the doors. The script to Beauty and the Beast became as natural to me as breathing. I had always wondered how it was possible to memorize a two and a half hour play, but I began to see it was easy. Deon was a lovely partner, who worked at my pace rather than surging ahead and expecting me to follow.

Sarah became my confidant again and we spoke every night. I dismissed Liam as a 'bad idea that should have never happened,' and she pretended to believe me, even on nights when I didn't believe myself.

And in class, Liam behaved like I was any other student. He spoke to me only when I needed direction and he was emotionless. His eyes were dark, cold and distant. We no longer caught each other's gazes in class, no longer took separate directions just to sneak to my dorm.

With Liam not taking up all of my time, I began to make friends with my classmates, learning to trust them on and off stage. It was a slow process, of course, to learn to talk civilly to the girls that had shunned me for the first half of the semester. But now that Liam ignored me, their jealousy ebbed away, and we soon spent hours giggling in the hallways and reciting the same lines over and over until we were sick of them.

The girls showed me websites to submit for auditions on my own, and we often spent lunch hours tailoring each other's resumes and emailing casting calls to each other. Although no one emailed me back, it felt like a good start; like I could do this on my own.

I was happy. I was afraid to admit it at first. I was afraid that things were too good and would disappear as quickly as they had appeared. But even Dad began to comment on the change in my manner, my speech and my mood. I was finally living the dream that I had longed for since I first set foot in the academy as a child, and being involved with the headmaster had never been part of it anyway.

One morning, however, everything began to change.

The strands of the well-known pop song reached my ears before I even fully opened the door to the theater. The lights in the audience were off, and the only light on was the main light on the stage. Porsche was flying through a dance routine, and attempting to cover the song as well, although her voice wasn't quite the same as the pop singer.

She looked different than her ballet persona; her limbs moving with speed instead of slow grace and her red hair was flying all over the place. Porsche was gorgeous, in every way that counted, and I briefly wondered if Liam had told me the truth about their relationship. Or perhaps I had just been a pawn in the game.

"Sorry, I didn't know the stage was in use," I said, turning to go when she spotted me at the end of the song.

She smiled, panting slightly and came to the front of the stage. "No, no. I have an audition later so I thought I'd practice. But I would get slaughtered if anyone knew I was taking the stage from students. Hop on up." She went to get a water bottle, gesturing to me to come up the steps. "How are you, Amy? I heard you were sick a while back."

I blushed, looking away. The look that she gave me told me that she knew the full story behind it.

"What are you auditioning for?" I asked, changing the subject.

She smiled. "Broadway."

"But you're a ballerina! And a star ballerina!" I protested.

She shrugged. "Sure. But you can't be a ballerina forever. Like being a model, you age out of it fast, or you get injured and have no backup plan. In musical theater, there are parts galore for an older crowd. So once ballet is over, I can continue to dance. And maybe sing. But I doubt it."

"It sounded good." I offered her an encouraging smile. "Are you here to teach too?" Porsche guest taught the dance classes whenever she was in town, often jet-lagged and right off a plane. Her life was something I could only dream of, and it gave me hope, that even with a beeping watch reminding me to take my pills, I could still have a good career.

"Possibly. Auditions can take five minutes or keep you waiting two hours, so it depends when I get back. I'm hoping to be back in time for the five o'clock class, but the audition is at three, so who knows."

"Wow," I said, awed despite myself. "Are you excited?"

She shrugged again, reaching to tie her hair back. "The average working performer goes to ten auditions before getting one job, so you can't dwell too much on all of them. My stats are a little higher, maybe one in five, but still not a reason to put all my eggs in one basket."

"Oh," I said as I reached the stage. "I guess my stats are about 1 in 1 right now."

"The only audition you've done is for here?" she asked, surprised. "Really?"

"Really." I shrugged. "Stroke of luck. Or…a little more"

"You have to come with me!" she said abruptly, and my mouth hit the floor.

"What? No, I can't. I mean, I haven't submitted, I haven't rehearsed, I don't even know what it's for, I don't have a resume, I don't…"

"I'll make a call." Liam's deep voice surprised me from the wings. He approached from stage left, and unconsciously, I froze. I wasn't quite sure what we were supposed to say or do now.

"That isn't necessary," I managed, finding my voice. Despite the fact that his voice was kind, it made me angry. I didn't need any more handouts. It was the first time we had spoken one on one since it had happened. Mostly, he just barked directions at me from across the stage, and I obeyed them without answering.

"This industry is all about whom you know, Amy," Porsche said, a gentle smile on her face as she came to stand beside me. "And getting your foot in the door, however you can. Lots of people are talented, so you have to stand out."

"But..." I started to protest.

"If you didn't come here to try and succeed, why did you come?" Liam's voice had taken on that cold distant chill that I used to know him so well for. There was no warmth between us, no light, and no connection anymore. "Who's the casting director?" he addressed Porsche without so much as meeting my eyes.

"It's Shannon," she said, taking another sip of her water. "Which means she will needlessly remind me about the time I tripped in front of her."

"At least she'll see you." There was the warmth I remembered, but it wasn't directed at me. "Amy, you'll go with Porsche after your English class this afternoon. If you're feeling up to it." His eyes bore into me, but I held my ground.

"I'm fine," I said.

"Just for an acting call," Porsche tried to reassure me. "We won't force you to be a triple threat yet. Use the monologue you did for Beauty, it'll be perfect."

"Right." I nodded, my heart hammering in my chest. I knew he was right. They both were. This industry was as much about whom you knew as what you could do. So, deciding to take the high road, I nodded. "Thank you."

"What am I calling Shannon for?" Liam said, just as he turned to leave. "She's probably casting 80 things right now."

"Gatsby," Porsche replied, rolling her eyes. "I told you about 60 times." He raised an eyebrow.

"And you think you'd be a good Daisy Buchannan, then?"

"No, but Myrtle Wilson played by Porsche De Ritter has a nice ring to it." She winked at him, and he sighed, heading out.

"Break a leg. And Amy?" He barely looked at me. "Try not to waste the whole day telling everyone. You have school work to focus on."

"I'll do that," I replied, trying hard not to glare after him. He didn't look back, strolling off as if he had said a pleasant goodbye. When the tension in the air cleared with his exit, I cleared my throat.

"Gatsby?" I turned to Porsche in shock. "That's a huge production! Everyone in the school submitted for that at least twice. I think I submitted three times. Isn't it set to star a Hollywood superstar as Gatsby himself? And that's Shannon Valirie casting it? Didn't she cast Wicked and Phantom and...." I could barely catch my breath.

"Sure is," she grinned. "You read it?"

"I read it at home, by myself. I know the story. But..."

"Then you'll do fine," she replied. "Most actors have so many auditions they show up without a clue, anyway. But don't focus on that now. You came here to rehearse something else, I think."

"I did." I nodded, but suddenly, Beauty and The Beast didn't seem so important.

The day went by in a blur. It took every ounce of concentration I had to not think about it. Even though I managed to get through class and rehearsal and no one asked why I was acting like a space cadet, I still couldn't help but look at the clock every ten seconds. At least watching the clock kept me from watching out for Liam.

It still happened, much to my annoyance. I found myself quickly searching a room for him, or my heart skipping half a beat when he walked in. If our eyes happened to meet, they still lingered for half a second, but now, they held no warmth.

At exactly 2:55, I met Porsche at the front of the school.

"Do you think this is ok?" I asked, gesturing down to my outfit. "I mean, do I have time to change?"

"They want to see you, not your wardrobe. You look fine," she assured me, placing a hand on my shoulder. It was only then that I noticed the band-aid on her arm.

"Are you ok?" I asked, pointing to it as we began to walk. It was a 25 minute walk to the audition studio.

"Sure." She shrugged, pulling her sleeve over her hand and putting her thumb through one of the fashion-placed holes in the cuff. "A little infection a couple days ago. Nothing that an IV wouldn't take care of."

"I know that story. You're still on AZT, right? Nothing yet?"

"I am." She looked to me. "It's nice to have someone who actually understands the medical jargon."

"Yeah." I nodded, giving her a grin. "It is."

Porsche took a deep breath, looking me up and down before continuing. "It doesn't really matter anyway. I'll live my life and then when it comes to its natural end, Liam turns me."

I knew that. In the back of my mind, I had known that about her. He had told me. But hearing her say it out loud was still shocking.

"But why would you go through all of it?" I asked. "Once the disease descends into full blown AIDS, it's going to be brutal, and we all know that."

"Because I will have all of eternity to be immortal," she replied. "And a very short time to remember what being mortal is."

I didn't really know what to say to that, how to continue this conversation. It was surreal to be talking completely seriously about vampires.

"He's a good person, Amy..." she started, and that's when I cut her off.

"I really don't want to talk about it, Porsche," I snapped, shaking my head. "It happened, and it's over. And it's a lot more complicated than him simply being...what he is."

"I get that," her voice was still gentle, despite my tone.

"Well, you don't, because you get to be immortal when it's done," I replied.

She glanced at me, sharply. "And you want that?"

"No!" The thought had never even crossed my mind. "Can we talk about something else?"

"Sure." She looked away and we lapsed into silence until we hit the audition studio. It was small, smaller than I had been expecting, and there were very few people in the waiting room when we walked in.

"Professional auditions are smaller," Porsche told me, as she signed us in. "You usually have to have a resume a mile long and be personally known by the director."

"Lucky me," I said, as I took a seat. The other two people in the waiting room were beautiful male actors, probably not much older than me. I was grateful for the fact that we didn't have to sit there with someone competing directly with us, and so I settled in comfortably, watching them warm up. "Are you guys dancers?" I asked when I had caught their gaze one too many times.

"Yes." One of them, the more beautiful of the two, I felt, nodded. He had dark hair and light blue eyes that contrasted beautifully with his dark skin. "Are you?"

"No." I shook my head. "She is, though," I said, indicating Porsche, who uncrossed her legs and smiled, although it was tight-lipped.

"Braedon and I know each other," she said. "Braedon, this is Amy, the scholarship winner of the Academy this year."

"Well, well, well. Looks like Liam is still picking them pretty." He held his hand out to me, and I shook it, but immediately felt uneasy. There was something about the way he looked at me that I didn't like, as if he were judging me. I felt myself sit up straighter. I may have gotten here on a scholarship, but I had talent too. If there was one thing I still trusted about Liam, it's that he wouldn't have thrown the school to the wolves by casting a horrible actor even if I hadn't been the best one.

Porsche had been right about the waiting. It was agonizing. Despite being the only four in the waiting room, it was over an hour and a half before someone appeared at the door. Exiting just ahead of her was another group of what appeared to be dancers, tired and sweaty.

"All right, next group? Dancers, you'll be at dance call for two hours, so if you need to call anyone, do it now."

"Wait for me?" Porsche asked, as she stood, putting her stuff away. "You'll probably be called in and done before me."

"Uh...sure," I said, shrugging. She was just about to leave when she turned back.

"Shoot. Amy, be a dear and text Liam, tell him I certainly won't be able to teach today," she said it without even waiting for an answer. If she had gotten one, however, it would have been a frustrated growl from me. And I'm sure she knew that. This was a set up.

I slid my phone out of my pocket, scrolling down the contacts. Liam was still saved as 'Lover,' lest anyone find my phone when I left it lying around. My heart was hammering more than before. The nervousness of the audition combined with the fact that I now had to make contact with Liam. The only audition I had even done was with him and the only acting advice I had ever gotten was through him as well. Doing all of this alone was weighing heavily on me.

At the last second, I hit *call* instead of *SMS* and brought the phone up to my ear. It rang once, twice, three times, and I was hoping it would go to voice mail when Liam picked up.

"Hi, it's Amy," I said, the words tumbling out.

"Yes?" He sounded annoyed and I could hear the background noise of the school hallways.

"Porsche just went in for dance call, so she wants me to tell you she won't be able to teach tonight. And I'm uh...still waiting." My heart was beating so hard that I could barely get the words out. I felt sweat dripping down my back and I knew my voice was trembling. I was frustrated at myself for feeling this way, but no matter how many calming thoughts I tried to think, nothing was helping.

"Ok." Liam sounded gentler now, and the noise in the background faded. "Is everything alright?"

"Um, yeah." Suddenly, I didn't want to hang up on him. I didn't want to shut out his voice. "Thank you. For this."

"Not a problem," he replied, and I heard a note of concern. "If you don't feel like walking back, Amy, please do call me, I can certainly arrange for you to be picked up."

"I'm fine. Really." But even listening to him was slowing the beat of my heart. I heard a noise and looked up, to see someone standing at the door again, looking directly at me. "Got to go." I hung up the phone abruptly and shoved it into my pocket.

"Are you Amy?" the woman at the door asked, and I nodded. "Come right this way."

"Sure," I squeaked out, standing up. I followed her down a winding hallway, which seemed endless. She didn't say a word to me, didn't turn back to make sure I was right behind her. I closed my eyes as we walked and I tried to remember the lines to the monologue I had burned into my brain.

She opened a door, leading me into a small room. Behind a table were three other people; two men and a woman.

"Sorry for the wait, we needed to see a bit of the dancers first," the other woman said, reaching out to shake my hand. "I'm

Shannon. It's nice to meet you. I saw your submission a week ago and thought you looked like a perfect Daisy. But I didn't realize who you were." She addressed her panel, "People, Amy is the new scholarship winner at Leopard Academy."

"Oh." They gave me a smile and I felt anger flare. Was that how I was going to be referred to as for the rest of my career—as a by-product of Liam's success? Perhaps letting him get me this audition was not such a good idea. If Shannon had liked my look, hadn't she been planning to call me anyway? I scanned my memory quickly, trying to remember if I had left my phone off at any point or forgot to check my junk email. "And what do you have prepared for us, Amy?"

"Uh…" I paused, taking a deep breath. "A monologue, one that we are working on in school."

Shannon waved her hand, indicating I should head to the center of the room and start. Starting was the hardest part, and it took several breaths before the words came out of my mouth. But once they did, they flowed. I knew this monologue, I knew Beauty's emotions and feelings as well as I knew my own. The fact that the people were unfamiliar to me and that the staging was different didn't bother me. I leapt into it, not holding back anything. *Make Strong Choices*. Liam's motto echoed in my head, and when I finished, I found myself on the ground, Beauty's tears pouring from my eyes.

There was a silence from the panel, and then they nodded.

"Thank you, Amy. We'll be making our choice in the next few days and will be in touch."

"Uh…that's it?" I asked, surprised. "No cold read?"

"That's all. You're still in school, right?" Shannon asked.

I nodded. "Yes, but…"

"So if we're interested, we'll talk to Liam. Thank you." She gave me a look that clearly indicated I was to leave.

I got up, turning my back quickly.

"Thank you," I said, rushing out of the room. My heart was running a marathon again, and I wasn't sure how to feel. I knew auditions were supposed to be like that, but that one felt wrong. I had caught the condescending tone they had used when referring to me as the scholarship winner; that I had only gotten before their panel by Liam's influence. And they clearly weren't impressed by that.

Porsche was another half hour, and the silence of the waiting room almost killed me, the thoughts running through my head like wild fire.

"How'd it go?" she asked, when she came out.

I shrugged. "I don't know. They didn't let me do anything besides the monologue. And they looked at me like I was a reality show winner."

"Ah, Amy, it doesn't mean anything." She shrugged. "Shannon's just like that. She knows talent when she sees it."

"Whatever. I just want to go home," I replied, gathering up my stuff.

"Sure." She checked her phone, and then picked up her own coat. "Are you alright?"

"I'm fine." Once we were outside, the cool breeze hit me like a calming wave. "I just…I don't know how to feel. Schizophrenic is probably the right answer. One second, I was happy to be there,

130

and the next second, I was angry for not getting it on my own. And then I was…"

"Life of a performer," Porsche said, with a shrug. "A different emotion every second and it's never half-assed either."

"I just…I wish I had gotten it on my own," I said, and she draped an arm around my shoulders.

"Don't worry about it. The important part is they saw you today."

"Right," I replied, although I didn't believe her.

The sun was just setting when we got back to school, half way down the horizon. Porsche bid me goodbye at the entrance, heading to the dancer's wing to spend the night. I thanked her and turned in the opposite direction, glad for the chance of silence. It didn't last long however.

Liam was stalking down the empty hallway with haste, and I knew exactly where he was going. As much as I wanted to ignore him, I couldn't. I nodded to him as we passed each other, and he nodded back. Already, his eyes were dark and he was pale, and I knew he didn't have long. I thought I would escape without a word, leaving him to enter the half hidden door, when suddenly he called out to me.

"Amy!"

Rolling my eyes, I backtracked a few paces.

"Yes?"

"The door's locked." He jiggled the handle a few more times. "Damn Peter, that forgetful man."

I glanced out the window. The sun was almost set, and I could see it in Liam's face that he didn't have much time. "Uh…"

"Please go to reception and ask them for a spare set of keys. Tell them it's for me, I'll call ahead."

The condescending tone of *the scholarship winner* was still in my head, and part of me didn't want to help him. But he met my eyes, gritting his teeth, and I could see the pain of transformation already taking place. I nodded and headed swiftly down the hall. Getting the key was no problem. Students got locked out all the time and needed the master key. I brought it to Liam within minutes, and he took it, gratefully.

"Did it go well today?" he asked, as he slipped it in the lock.

"Yeah, except for the part where they sounded like they would have called me in anyway. They treated me like a reality show winner, Liam."

He raised an eyebrow as the door opened.

"But they saw you," he said. "And they saw your talent."

"That's what Porsche said," I replied, and he smiled. For a moment, that smile floated me back to a time when things were different.

"Well, she's a smart one. It's just the way Shannon is." He shrugged. "And talent like yours deserves to be seen, Amy, no matter how you get there."

"By lying and pretending to be someone I'm not?" I accused him, and he glared at me, handing me back the key without another word. We held each other's gaze a moment, and then he slammed the door in my face. Rolling my eyes, I went to hand the key back to reception. I wanted nothing more than a hot shower and sleep.

But, as I walked back to my dorm room, a part of me glanced back where I had left Liam. Regardless of the outcome, I had my first professional audition today. It was a dream come true, and it was because of him.

Sighing, I locked my door and headed to the shower. Dreams didn't always come true the way you wanted them to.

CHAPTER 14: LIAM

My phone rang at 8am, just as I got out of the shower. Porsche was sprawled across my bed, still fast asleep, so I grabbed it and headed back into the bathroom. Since she was here, last night's transformation did not involve chains and a basement cell the entire night. Instead, we had driven over to the big city and taken advantage of a night club that would not miss a few pieces of riffraff. I hadn't had a party night like that in quite a while, and it felt good to return to the life that had made me. But when the lights came on at the club, and the afterhours club closed their doors, we had no choice but to make our way back home; leaving me only enough time to shower and change before I was expected in morning classes. Porsche, however, informed me she had nowhere to be, and climbed into my bed. Oh, to be human again. My head was still pounding from the loud music and the booze; keeping the cravings at bay just long enough to lure someone outside.

There had been no bodies last night, only semi-drained victims that would find their way to a hospital. But I still felt more energized than I had been in a long time. Human blood gave me new life as the sun rose. My human companion however, had seemed the opposite. Normally, my antics when I was half drunk and high on blood kept her in stitches. But last night, she seemed nothing but annoyed with me, playing on her phone and refusing the long line of partners who lined up, wanting a dance with her. When the sun finally began to rise, she practically dragged me to the car, mid-transformation. The hour long ride back hadn't been much fun either.

Her mood had gotten to me, and while I felt energized, I found the atmosphere that had once made me so happy didn't do a thing for my attitude. The endless supply of women and booze didn't feel like quite the reprieve it usually did, and I was glad to finally return to the school.

"Hello," my voice came through a bit louder than I intended, and I turned on the tap to drown it out.

"Liam, darling, it's been too long."

"Hello, Shannon," I said, glancing at myself in the mirror. Years ago, Shannon had cast me in a few movies before moving back to her first love, theater. I didn't particularly like her. She was full of attitude and ego … but then, so was I.

"I got your pint-sized package yesterday," she said, and I could hear her flipping through papers on the other side of the phone. "Very impressive. When she walked in, I thought for sure there was only one reason you'd pick her. But she's got some talent as well."

"Do you really think I'm so shallow, Shannon?" I asked with a smirk on my face as I reached for a towel to rub my hair dry. I put the phone down, pressing speaker phone and turned off the tap. "That I would put the whole school in jeopardy to cast a pretty girl?"

"That's the Liam I know," she replied, and it made me set my jaw.

She was right, of course. Beautiful women were what got me into this whole mess in the first place and I'd once rather have a blond on my arm that couldn't form a sentence than a bespectacled brilliant nerd.

"And so, since you know me so well, what's the answer to the question you are about to ask?" I wrapped the towel around my waist and sprayed on some cologne.

"The answer is of course, yes. I'm going to take Gatsby on the tour circuit in two months. Rehearsals start next week. Amy can join the chorus."

135

"As an understudy?" I asked, leaning against the counter.

"No, just a chorus girl—for the party scenes and such. She'll have a few lines, maybe. But I'll bill her as on loan from your school—it'll be good publicity for the Academy. We'll do a whole 'introducing' thing, as if your school turns out students directly ready for the professional world."

"If rehearsals start next week, she won't be on loan," I replied, calculating how many days were left in the term. "This is her final semester here so she'll finish the final show and then leave with you...and I don't know if she's ready, Shannon. There was talk of her being here another year. You know how it is with people who peak too soon."

"Or she won't be the first to drop out of school for a show," Shannon purred. "Full union rates, full contract."

"Right." I glanced up at the mirror. I looked fully human now, if not a little tired, but I felt like I was walking through a fog. I squinted, trying to focus. Shannon was right, of course, the publicity with that kind of announcement would launch this school to a whole new level of success. It was Peter's dream to bring the school to a level where it would be recognized as the best training academy in the world.

And it would be a convenient way to sever ties with Amy. My chest ached at the thought of her. She was angry and cold, but I was no better. Her judgmental actions had ripped my heart out, and I cursed myself for getting involved. How could I have thought that someone in this damn world would actually understand enough to be able to look past it? The truth was, I was still the Hollywood Hunk and that's all they ever wanted. If it came with complications, women took off faster than a jetpack.

136

If she was gone from the school, and I confirmed it now, then I killed two birds with one stone. I'd be free of the awkwardness every time we saw each other and the school would soar to a new level of success. I could replace her as Beauty in an instant.

"I'll talk to her," I said as I opened the door. To my surprise, Porsche was stretched on the floor in the splits, her dancer's body fully folded over as she stretched. She glanced at me, and I raised an eyebrow, watching her. She looked pale in the dawn light, her jaw set as her limbs contorted into poses only a dancer could pull off. "Hey, I also sent you Porsche De Ritter. She's a dancer. My first scholarship winner."

"I remember her," Shannon replied, and her tone dropped. Porsche glanced at me, and I shrugged. "I'm holding dance callbacks next week and I'm going to call her back."

"Porsche's the prima ballerina at the Russian National," I snapped, my tone reflecting the look Porsche gave the cell phone. "Are callbacks really necessary?"

"I'm worried about her stamina, Liam. Skinny little dancers like her can pull off a grand ball but 8 shows a week is a different matter. Even in the audition, it raised a red flag. Talk to your girl and get back to me by tomorrow."

"Right." I hung up the phone then, and crossed my arms, leaning against the bathroom doorway.

"Did she want Amy?" Porsche asked, as she slowly drew her limbs in.

"Forget Amy, what's going on with you?" I didn't miss the look of pain on her face as she came back into first position.

"I've been up all night, Liam, relax."

137

"Well, you weren't up all night when you auditioned, so why is Shannon going on about a lack of stamina?" I asked, heading to my dresser to pull out clothes.

"Uh," Porsche replied, sitting on the bed and rotating both her ankles with her hands. I heard her joints pop from across the room and gave her a look. "Because Shannon is a helpless liar who will say anything to get her way and you know it? I swear, if she didn't have so much power, I would never even look at her again."

"Porsche…" My worst fear, looking into her face, was that she would do something incredibly stupid, which I knew she was capable of. She wanted to be human, I understood that. But insisting on waiting until her dying breath to be changed into a vampire was one of the stupidest moves she could make. We weren't always together. We couldn't be and I feared that one day, something would happen and I wouldn't be able to get to her in time. "What do you know?"

"I know that all dancers age out and I'm jet-lagged, running on about an hour's sleep. So you need to stop worrying. Now, did they want Amy?"

"They did," I said, pulling on a shirt. "For a chorus role though. Rehearsals start soon, and then the show is on tour, so she certainly won't have another year here. But Shannon is willing to do a partnership agreement. It's an amazing boost for the school. It could help give us what we need to actually rank as top in the world."

"And you won't have to awkwardly stare at each other in class," she pointed out, standing up. "Industry break-ups are always awkward."

"It's not awkward," I snapped, turning to distract myself. "She'll stop looking at me like a lost puppy dog, and the school will get a boost. Win."

"Except killing herself at rehearsal there, when she has a lead role here, to just play a chorus girl and possibly get stuck there forever, isn't the best advice in the world." Porsche went to her purse, rummaging around for what I assumed were her pills. "Did you think of that?"

"I can't hold their hands!" I protested, turning back to her. "I got her the audition, I got her the contact, and the rest is up to her. I need this for the school … whether she's stuck in the chorus forever or not."

"She's better than that," the dancer replied, quietly. "And she doesn't have a lot of time to waste in the chorus."

"That's not really my concern." I said, trying to ignore the look she was giving me. Porsche met my eyes, reading my face without even trying.

"You don't want her to go, do you?" she asked, not seeming surprised at all.

I scoffed at it. "Of course I want her to go. Why exactly do I want a judgmental clingy teenager hanging around here?" I asked, and Porsche smiled slightly.

"You don't remember when I found out about you? Shields aren't supposed to ally themselves with anyone. We're brought up to believe vampires are terrible evil creatures. It took me a while to get over my prejudices and beliefs about you too."

"You didn't run screaming from the room in terror, either," I said. "Making me feel like I was some sort of monster."

139

"We're all some sort of monster," she pointed out, and we fell into silence a moment, locking eyes. Eventually, I looked away, not wanting to address the fact that she could read me like an open book.

"Now, are you going to teach for me today, since you're taking up space?"

Porsche rolled her eyes, swallowing the antiretroviral meds without water, and rising, heading to the shower herself.

"Whatever, Liam," she replied, but the slamming of the door told me she meant much differently. I rolled my eyes, letting the towel drop to fully get dressed.

She had a point, of course. Shannon did have a tendency to make sure her chorus performers felt lower than the ticket takers at the theaters they performed at. And Beauty and the Beast would be attended by scouts across the country; the year end show always was. But at the moment, thinking of how Amy had bolted from the room that night, I really didn't care.

I tried to rationalize with myself, jogging my memory of all the people I had seen fall because they were thrown into the world too early. They had shown too much promise at an audition and were given a lead role in a professional setting without training or discipline. Their talent faltered, their stamina failed, or they got too used to the easy money and fell down the wrong path. The industry was a hard world to live in and if you didn't come up slowly, your peak would also be your downfall.

Except I couldn't forget the memory of her audition. She had stood out from the crowd and it was more than just the way she looked, or the way she smelled. Amy had the most raw talent that I had ever seen. From the moment she opened her mouth, I was mesmerized, barely able to get the lines out myself.

And classes were just awkward. Porsche was right. I had to resist not meeting her eyes to give her a special glance; resist not looking forward to lunchtime when we used to meet. Her supple lips nearly killed me every time she licked them. And the memory of her body, lean and smooth, as my hands had run over it, was almost enough to make me groan out loud.

I finished buttoning my shirt, and ran a bit of gel through my hair, satisfied with the reflection in the mirror. The sooner I was rid of all of this, the better it would be for all of us.

CHAPTER 15: LIAM

"Are you serious?"

I had called Amy into my office to deliver the news of the phone call. Shannon had faxed over the contract, clear in her assumption that we would accept.

"Yes, you wowed them, just as you wowed me," I replied, but there was no warmth in my voice as I said it. She narrowed her eyes, watching as I got a pen and put the contract in front of her.

"What about next year? I thought that it was pretty much decided I would get an extra year."

"Well, now you won't," I snapped, trying to hide the nagging feeling in my chest. Raw talent was just half the game. Everyone knew that.

"But still, this is huge."

Even if we weren't really on speaking terms, her happiness was flowing out of her like a river. And I felt bad not offering her more advice. She wanted help, and that's what I was supposed to be there for.

"So you accept?" I asked, and she looked up, detecting the tone in my voice.

"Of course, I accept. Why wouldn't I?"

"No reason," I said, with a shrug. "Only that it's a small role. And I know Shannon. She's not particularly fond of people rising through the ranks. And, if you take this, you're gone. There's no coming back here if you find Hollywood too nasty for you."

"But it can be done. Aaron Douglas was an extra for years before he was a lead. And so was Ricky Gervais," she replied, listing off names on her fingers. "I can do it. And I can do it on my own, Liam. They would have called me in for an audition without your influence. They told me so themselves."

"And you believe everything the audition panel tells you? That alone screams that you have no idea what the industry is like, Amy. If they don't like you—you make one wrong move—they'll drop you and blacklist you faster than you can cry for help. And sometimes, you don't even know you've made the wrong move. For God's sake, you didn't even know that when the panel said 'thank you' they meant 'goodbye.' In the mock auditions, you stood there like a deer in headlights until your instructor dismissed you."

"That's not true. I knew that!" she protested, glaring at me.

"Fine." I looked over at my wall, glancing at anything that would keep me from meeting her eyes. "Then sign it. Once the announcement is official, and they don't back out, we'll credit you for graduation here."

"Do you think…"

Suddenly I heard the doubt in her voice. I looked up and saw all the traces of anger were gone, as she looked over the contract and then back at me.

"Do you think it's a bad idea?"

I sighed, looking back at her. "You can do whatever you want, Amy. You've been doing that all along."

"What's that supposed to mean?" Her eyes flared angrily again, and I cocked an eyebrow at her. I almost smiled as I realized how alike we were; this constant back and forth of extreme emotions tumbling out faster than we could get a hold of them.

"Do you want me to make my own list? You left your father when he wanted the best for you at home. You chose to pursue a career that one out of every million make it at when you had a hundred other options. You're now choosing a gig that is peanuts. And you...me..." I sputtered, unable to control my anger. "Just sign it and leave, Amy."

Her eyes widened, and I saw fear in them, for the first time. I had never seen her look at me with true fear; not like this, not even on the night I revealed myself to her.

"I'll read it myself and get it back to you later," she said standing and taking the contract. "I trust I'm allowed to do that, without you holding my hand?"

"Go." I flicked my wrist at her, indicating the closed door. Without another word, she picked up her bag and left, making sure to slam the door on her way out. I buried my head in my hands, sighing. Two women slamming doors in my face within the space of two hours had to be some sort of record.

Why in the world was this proving to be so difficult? A year ago—hell, even six months ago—I wouldn't have thought twice about selfishly sacrificing anyone if it meant I could be freed from this hell I was living in. But whether I liked it or not, Amy had changed something in me. If the school got the boost it needed, I could settle back into easy retirement, live off the money it made and never have to deal with humans again. I would secure everyone's future.

But I also knew Amy would go far if connected with the right people, and Shannon was the opposite of the right person. Shannon's performers became trapped with her, often taking the easy way out and staying in her shows forever; always hovering as a working actor; right below fame. Amy was right, though, if anyone could break free of that trap, it was her.

Still, working for Shannon was better than being stuck in school, and I knew that was a fact. Amy had to face challenges all her life and I knew she would be strong in the face of this one. After all, I had gotten out of Shannon's 'curse,' and I didn't believe I was anywhere near as talented as Amy was.

I sighed again, rubbing my hands with my face. There was, of course, the real reason I had let my anxiety about the situation slip.

I didn't want her to go. I tried to convince myself I did, a thousand times, but I didn't. I didn't want her to fly away forever, and never come back to me. Despite what had happened, the way she had made me feel when we were together was something I would likely never forget. She had changed something in me. She'd made my soul come alive again.

I wasn't going to hold her back. I wasn't going to let my fears slip through again. She knew what she was doing and I couldn't deny that I knew she had the talent to go far. So if this was to be the end, so be it. I had to let her go.

CHAPTER 16: AMY

I closed the door before sinking to the floor in my room. Tears streamed down my cheeks. I tucked my head down against my knees, sobbing as if my heart would break. There were so many things I was feeling, it was impossible to figure out why exactly I was crying. I was excited. I was scared. I was hurt.

I had never expected to get the role, and I thought I hadn't wanted it without Liam's help. But talking to him just before going into the audition hall had given me the calm I needed to carry on, and I'm sure I couldn't have done it without him.

And before all of this, I had looked forward to another year here. I was still stumbling with what 'stage left' and 'stage right' meant, trying to remember they were the opposite of the normal view. I had just learned that 'corpse' meant to break character, not to fall down dead, during a scene. And I still felt like there were a million things going through my head.

And Liam ... he had been so harsh. It was clear he wanted me to go. He wanted me to leave the school. I hadn't realized how much I had missed him until he called me into his office and the memories we had in there came flooding back. A very small part of me had hoped he was calling me in to reconcile.

I didn't care what he was now. It didn't matter to me. He was what he was, and I accepted that. But the distance that had grown between us seemed too great to ever cross; to go back to the way things were.

And why else had I come here if not to pursue my dreams? This is exactly what I wanted to do with my life and here it was, being offered to me on a plate. I would be an idiot not to take it; not to move forward and leave this school forever.

Wiping my tears away, I went to take a sip of water and look over the contract. I was to be a chorus girl with few lines and the possibility of more as the show went on. It signed me on exclusively for three years which seemed like a long time, but maybe that was normal. The show's run was to be a year, so maybe it would be extended.

Opening my desk drawer, I slipped the contract in, and headed to the bathroom then splashed water on my face. It was time to head to rehearsal for Beauty. I could deal with this when I got back.

I locked my door and headed down the hallway. My mind was still back in Liam's office, replaying the situation over and over again. I was so stuck in the moment that I didn't notice the woman standing in front of me until I bumped right into her.

"Oh my God, I'm so sorry!" I said, as I stumbled back. She was beautiful, tall and long limbed, with dark hair and dark eyes that were exotic looking. When her eyes met mine, I took a step back. I went to a school full of beautiful people and she was possibly one of the most beautiful women I had ever seen.

"It's alright, Amy." When she spoke, her words curled around her tongue, a liquid French accent pouring out. "One such as you has a lot to keep her pre-occupied."

"How do you know my name?" I asked, surprised, and she smiled slightly.

"Everyone knows the scholarship winner," she said gently. "You are famous around this school."

"Oh...uh...thank you," I said, blushing. "Can I help you? Are you lost?"

"No." She shook her head, a twinkle in her eye. "I am an old friend of Liam's, merely here to observe."

Of course you are, I thought, a rush of anger flooding my veins. There seemed to be a lot of beautiful women floating around this school who were 'old friends of Liam's.' Glancing at my reflection in the window beside us, I wondered how I could have ever competed. With my eyes red from crying, and my hair in a messy pony tail, I felt like a hot mess compared to this beautiful woman. *That's fine* I thought, trying to keep my face neutral. *Liam can have his harem of women now that I'm out of the picture.*

"All right, well..." I said, looking past her to the door where I needed to go. "It was good to meet you..." I paused, realizing I didn't know her name.

"Selene," she said, extending a long arm with long elegant fingers, perfectly manicured.

"Selene." I shook it, surprised at the coolness of it. My palms were sweaty in comparison, and I was annoyed that it seemed every aspect of this woman was perfect. "I really have to get to rehearsal."

"Of course," she said, nodding. "Best of luck...break a leg. Isn't that what they say here in the theater?"

"Yes." I gave her a small smile. "Nice to meet you." Brushing past her, I headed down the hallway. I pulled open the door to the theater and hurried inside.

CHAPTER 17: AMY

I woke up about three hours early on the day of my first rehearsal with Shannon. Even though I had only slept for a few hours, I felt wide awake.

Yesterday, in preparation, I had gone into the registrar's office to show my valid contract and sign the school's agreement for 'Premiere Performers.' It was a program put in place to deal with the school's working performers. It allowed students working in the industry to come in and out of lessons as their schedule permitted, provided that it did not interfere with the rehearsal schedule of the school. That was Liam's one policy. He believed you could catch up with everything else, but rehearsal, where you learned the most, was not to be missed. So I was to attend Shannon's rehearsals every morning, and Liam's Beauty and the Beast every afternoon; making up class work on the weekends. My father was appalled at first at the schedule and worried about everything. To my surprise, it had been Liam who had come to my rescue.

"What Amy needs for her acting career now is not more lessons. She's miles ahead of even the senior students in the school. Now she needs experience and contacts with the right people," he said to my father during a private meeting. "That was what this school was always designed for, and that is what we can give her. Amy is already well ahead of her mandatory credits. She was home-schooled well and could have graduated a year early, I'm sure. Her graduation and education are of no concern. She would be the first choice of any college in the country."

Dad had hesitated, but when he saw my midterm report, he relented. I knew he didn't agree with my dreams of being an actress, although I could see it in his eyes that he would cross that bridge when he came to it. At the moment, his primary concern was my graduation. However, when he left, I could only give Liam a look.

"I'm not doing you a kindness, Amy," he said, responding to my raised eyebrow. "I was simply telling the truth."

"That's a first for you, isn't it?" I snapped, and he couldn't quite hide the wounded look on his face. For a moment, I felt bad about it. I hadn't meant to snap at him like that, but it seemed every time I got close to him or someone near him, another thing came out that I didn't know about. This wasn't how relationships were supposed to be, and I knew it.

His face hardened a second later and he turned away.

"I'll see you at rehearsal tomorrow."

"Right," I replied and left.

Getting into the shower and letting the warm water wash away my fatigue, I scrubbed my hair thoroughly. I wanted everything to be perfect for my first day of rehearsal.

I chose to wear all black because I didn't know what my character would be like, and I slipped into my comfortable black sneakers. I pulled my hair back, but did full makeup and made sure my nail polish wasn't chipped.

Then, to finalize the look, I added a beanie hat and aviator sunglasses that I had gotten in a discount sale. Now, the image looking back at me was that of an actress; an artist.

I dreaded going to Beauty and The Beast rehearsal this afternoon; hearing Liam's voice command me from some dark corner of the auditorium. All I wanted was to go to Gatsby rehearsal and stay there forever.

I left twenty minutes earlier than I needed to, resolving to walk slowly and take my time. I had the script tucked under my arm and my headphones connected to my cell phone. In my excitement and need for distraction, I video-called Sarah as I walked.

"Amy?" Her face popped up on the screen, although it was blurry and dark. "What's the matter?"

"Nothing," I replied. "It's my first Gatsby rehearsal today."

"That's great, but uh, time change?" she said, settling back on her pillows. "You couldn't have called me on your lunch break?"

"By lunch I'll be either awesome or dead on the floor," I said, looking up briefly to make sure I knew where I was going.

She sighed, and then smiled, propping herself up more. "So? Have you memorized your lines?"

"Yeah. All four of them," I said, looking both ways and then crossing the street. "But I mean…It's not the number of lines you have, it's the number of scenes you're in. And I'm in a lot. In the background, but still."

Sarah laughed quietly, and then reached over to her nightstand to get some water. "I'm sure you'll be great. They cast you, didn't they? So it's not like they don't know how talented you are. Man, I can't believe this is happening to you, I'm so jealous."

"Don't be," I said. "Because as soon as I get in good and make connections, I'll slip your name in."

"Sweet." Sarah grinned. "Hey, what about the ballerina? Porsche? Did they take her, so at least you'll know someone there?"

"Uh…" I looked up to narrowly miss a lamp post. "If they did, I don't know about it. Dancers are usually separate anyway."

"Don't worry, you'll make new friends," Sarah promised. "What did Liam say?"

"He said…" I averted my eyes, looking elsewhere. "I don't know. It doesn't matter anymore, does it?"

"You miss him, eh?" Sarah asked and I shrugged.

"I miss…having someone to talk to. I mean, you're a million miles away and I can't always just whisper something to you. And with Liam, everything felt so comfortable, like we could read each other's minds. They call it chemistry in this industry."

"And what else do you miss?" Sarah quirked an eyebrow at me, and I rolled my eyes.

"Shut up," I said, and she laughed.

"Look, Amy, I'm exhausted. Call me if you have a nervous breakdown, hopefully on your lunch break."

I nodded. I was only a few feet from the studio now and my excitement was building.

I opened the door to the rehearsal building, trying to calm myself. I was breathing like I had just run a marathon and my heart was racing a million miles a minute. With shaky hands, I reached into my purse, pulling out a water bottle and taking a sip. Finally, I ducked into the washroom and redid my hair and lip gloss. When I was only 5 minutes early, I emerged, heading to the huge rehearsal hall where I could hear voices.

I was stunned by the amount of people crowded into it. They were separated into two groups and one of them was clearly more confident than the other. I quickly realized that the less confident group was probably the one I belonged to, full of extras and crowd fillers. In the middle of the room, however, was what caught my eye. Belonging to neither group, the dancers flexed and stretched into impossible positions. They were the most gorgeous of the two groups, their bodies lean and toned and their faces glowing as they moved. In the center of the room, I recognized the two guys from the audition, although their names escaped me. To my delight, Porsche was there as well, watching as one of them helped another girl with a twist. She stepped forward, giving advice and demonstrating with her own twist, which was flawless.

Not knowing anyone else, I stepped forward.

"Hi," I said, when there was a break in movement.

Porsche turned, smiling at me. "Hey Amy. How's it going?"

"Good. I didn't know you were going to be here."

"First rehearsal, everyone is, and then we separate later. Your stuff goes over there." She pointed to a corner where about a hundred bags and coats were gathered and I realized everyone was unburdened.

Sheepishly, I nodded. "Sure. What are...what are you guys for? Are you like extra talented parts of the crowd?" I asked and she smiled, with a shrug.

"Kind of. Gatsby is an extravagant man who throws lots of parties where performers entertain his guests. It'll be the first time it's done this way—part musical, part ballet. Makes the show a hell of a lot longer, but apparently better."

"Cool," I said.

Shannon came into the room, accompanied by her own entourage. Silence followed and I was aware that I was the only one making noise as I scrambled to put my stuff away.

She gave me a look, and I nearly dropped my bag, hustling over to the group of crowd fillers. Finally, when I was standing quietly, she spoke.

"Let's go from top to bottom and see what we come up with. No interruptions. Divide yourselves up."

Those were the only instructions she gave. Everyone seemed to be scrambling, knowing what to do. I looked around in confusion, and then reached out to grab Porsche as she went past. She winced on instinct, pulling her wrist back instantly. My eyes widened.

"I'm sorry, are you hurt? I just didn't know what to do, where do I go? How can we run the show when it's first rehearsal?"

She took my hand, pulling me to the other side of the room. "This is the way Shannon works. You run it in first rehearsal, do what feels right, and then she'll base it off what your character does," she hissed at me and reached down to pull up her sleeve. To my horror, I saw it was raw where I grabbed it.

"Porsche, are you getting ..." I trailed off. Lesions were an advanced sign of AIDS, and there was no way she could be that sick already.

"No. I slipped during a step, that's all." She pulled her thin sleeve down with a shrug. She didn't seem concerned, and I let it go, remembering that even if she was, it didn't matter. Liam would give her immortality.

Bitterly, I turned my attention back to rehearsal. I had no idea how I was supposed to proceed. My character only had 4 lines in the show, and all of them seemed to make her a fan girl of Gatsby. I played them over and over again in my head as I watched the scene go by. The first crowd scene, and my first line, was in the second scene. I decided that if my character were a fan girl of Gatsby, then she would always try to be close to him.

When the scene changed, I fixed my eyes on Gatsby, who was actually incredibly attractive. With dark hair and dark eyes that sparkled, he had natural warmth about him and a fantastic smile. It was not difficult to pretend to be obsessed with him.

"Oh, Mr. Gatsby," I said when the time came, making sure I was right beside him. He kept moving though, and so I decided to follow. "You truly are the greatest host, and your parties are soooo much fun."

"STOP!" To my horror, I heard Shannon's voice. Looking over to the table, where the panel sat, I saw her standing up, and she did not look happy.

"Uh..." I froze.

"Amy, do you know what upstaging is?" she asked, sternly, and I nodded.

"You are a crowd filler, Amy, not the center of attention. You are a chorus girl, not a lead, so blend into the chorus. Say your line from the back and if no one, especially Gatsby, hears you, then all the better."

"But..." I said, and Shannon sighed.

"Be part of the background noise. What you have to say isn't important."

My cheeks were burning as I nodded. I kept my head down, but I could feel that everyone was staring at me. I desperately wanted Shannon to start the rehearsal again. When she finally did, I breathed a sigh of relief.

My next line came after nearly half an hour. Following instructions from last time, I hid in the back. I had been excited about this line, because one of the leads would be speaking to me, over the crowd.

"Oh, Mr. Gatsby is over there. You can't miss him," I said, quietly.

"AMY!" Shannon's voice came again and I turned, stunned.

"Yes?"

"Nick Caraway is asking you an important question. Nick is a lead and I can't hear a word you are saying."

"But you said..." I answered, confused. Shannon rolled her eyes.

"Amy, if you can't figure out how to build character, then perhaps you need to stay at school longer."

I heard snickers around me, and I ducked my head. Tears threatened to fill my eyes.

"Right," I muttered and Shannon sighed, sitting back down.

"Continue."

It seemed everything I did was wrong. I was taught to never have my back to the audience, yet Shannon screamed at me when I didn't turn properly to leave. I thought I was supposed to be Gatsby's biggest fan, but we never even crossed each other's paths.

By the end of the rehearsal, I wanted nothing more than to collapse into a ball and cry. Everyone was glancing at me, yet no one said a word to me as I gathered my stuff. I turned to see if Porsche wanted to walk home with me, but she was deep in conversation with the other dancers.

Zipping up my coat, I headed out the door alone. My phone was blinking with several messages from Sarah, wanting to know how it went. Ignoring them, I shoved my hands into my pocket, ducking my head against the wind. The weather seemed a lot more miserable this afternoon, but perhaps that was just my attitude. I felt so lost and confused. No one else needed to be corrected in their actions. I thought I knew what I was doing, but it was clear I was well out of my depth.

I grabbed some lunch at the cafeteria; a quick sandwich that I unwrapped and ate in the hallway. I didn't even want to talk to my dad.

I was grateful to slip into the familiar theater, at school, and clamored on the stage where I knew my place. Liam and Deon were already there, with the rest of the cast. They had started half an hour earlier, allowing me time for lunch. One of the stage assistants was reading my lines, and I tapped her on the shoulder. She smiled and nodded, and I turned my attention to the scene.

"The soup is delicious."

"Only the best for you," they said in unison, and I burst into laughter, the first time I had laughed all morning. With Liam doing only one show, and directing the rest, I knew he wasn't as strong on the lines yet. Clearly, they had decided to do a run through. Sitting on the stage, as they weren't going through formal blocking, I fed them lines and let them reply together; each one helping the other when they got stuck. They sounded like a two-headed dragon, and the rest of the theater was soon giggling along with me.

"I love you ... Beast," I said, with a grin on my face as I closed the scene. The rest of the cast burst into applause. Even Liam met my eyes and smiled. It was the nicest we had been to each other in weeks, but I couldn't help it. I felt so relieved to be here and not screamed at every four minutes.

"Thank you, Deon," Liam said. "That helped, a lot."

"It got a pretty good reaction. Let's do the shows like that," Deon replied as he wandered over to me. "Hey Amy, how would you like to be double-teamed?"

"Whaaa?" My jaw fell open and he grinned, offering me a hand up.

"How was rehearsal with the pros?"

"I don't really want to talk about it," I said, and Liam looked over. The concern in his eyes was prominent, and it was a look I hadn't seen in a long while.

"What happened?" he asked softly. I was tempted for a moment not to tell him, but it all came tumbling out.

"Everything I did was wrong. Shannon did a full run through and told us to do what 'feels right.' But apparently everything I did felt wrong to her. She called me out every second."

"Shannon has some strange ways," Liam said. "Don't worry about it, Amy."

"But I..."

"She cast you and she doesn't even cast the chorus unless they are amazing," he assured me.

"Thanks," I replied, quietly. We met each other's eyes for a moment and I couldn't help but feel the urge to reach out and touch him again. Then the moment was broken by the flickering of the stage lights.

"So today is going to be a bit different," Liam said, as the rest of the cast gathered around. "We're running out of time, and I admit part of that is my fault. So we're just going to do a run through, scene by scene, once with Deon and then once with me. It'll help all of you, because you get two chances to work on things.

Now, I know Deon and I play very different Beasts. So I want you to react differently to each of us. Just do what feels right, and I'm positive it'll be just fine." His eyes met mine again and I smiled, softly.

"How late are we going to go tonight, with two run throughs?" Someone asked, and Liam answered without ever taking his eyes off mine.

"I guarantee you'll be done by sunset," he said, and I couldn't help but smirk. Our eyes met, sharing a private secret, and just for a moment, I moved my mouth, baring fake fangs at him with a hiss. He struggled to contain his laughter.

"All right, Deon, let's have you go first so that I can have a bit more time to frantically memorize," he said, and everyone laughed as he shooed us off stage to our respective places.

"I sure hope he's serious about finishing by sunset, I have an audition tonight," Deon said, as he stood beside me in the wings.

"I'll bet you money we'll be done by sunset," I said, turning to him. "What's your audition for?"

"TV," he said. "It would conflict, but I'm not going to get it. One role, open call. Every actor in the area will be trying. I'm just going to practice auditioning for when we're out there in the real world and have no choice." He smiled at me. "Although apparently you needed no pro audition practice."

"There's some sort of stigma attached to winning a scholarship here," I replied. "And it could be good or bad."

"Looks like it's good in this case," Deon said, as the lights dimmed and the opening music started.

159

They were very different Beasts, as Liam had mentioned, but I felt like it gave me more freedom. I tried a few things, timidly at first, and then with more courage the second time as Liam nodded approvingly at me. This rehearsal felt so much better, my character flowing through me.

At the end of the last scene, Liam took my hand, turning me toward the nearly empty audience.

"The multi-talented Amy, ladies and gentlemen," he said, and they applauded. I blushed, taking a clumsy curtsy.

"All right, that's it for today," he said, clapping his hands. "Everyone out and lock the door behind you. Amy, stay a bit longer to go over a few things?"

"Uh...". I glanced at the setting sun, raising an eyebrow. He held my gaze pleadingly, and so I shrugged. I guessed what was coming, but I was in too good of a mood to care.

I sat on the edge of the stage, dangling my legs and saying goodbye to the rest of the cast. When we were finally alone with the door locked, he spoke.

"You were spectacular today," he said softly, and I just shrugged, watching the sunset out of the window.

"Well, at least for half the day."

"Amy." He came to sit beside me. I could already see the beginning of the transformation in his face. "I wasn't there, although I'm sure I will hear it from Shannon later. But I will say this: your talent is beyond belief and everyone knows it. I have never seen anyone with such natural talent and ability. If your technical skills are a bit rusty, then that's fine. Most performers train for years before getting their first job. You know this industry is more than just talent."

"I just felt...like a fish out of water," I said, sighing. "Everything I did was wrong."

"Did she ever call you out on your acting ability? Or just your technical skills?"

"Just tech," I said, and he nodded.

"See."

A silence fell over us, and I turned to face him. I could already see his fangs starting to grow.

"Do you want to go?" I asked, and he sighed, shaking his head.

"No. If you're alright, I'd like to keep going. But only if you're alright, Amy. Because you being tired may help me, but not you."

Realizing he was talking about the quality of my blood at the moment, I took a deep breath.

"I'm tired, but...why? Can't we do this in the morning when you're not..."

"The show runs at 8pm at night, Amy," he said. "Under the Beast makeup, I'll be in full transformation. So I have to get used to feeling this way now."

"What about when you're the prince?" I asked, and he smiled.

"I'll have my own private dressing room, and Porsche the multi-talented will do my makeup."

"But with all those...humans...in the audience..." I said, and he stood up, grinning.

"I have two ways around that. The first is that yes, there will be private citizens and media in attendance. But they will be sold seats in the back row and even then, the prices will be so high, barely anyone will come. It's a media stunt, that's all."

"And the front row?" I asked, and he grinned.

"It's being billed as a charity event. Rich snobs will purchase a ticket to donate to a child; a sick child who wants more than anything to see their favorite actor up close and personal. Win win."

I laughed out loud. It was genius, even I had to admit it. With rows and rows of excited, infected children, Liam would be fine.

"But what's the second way?" I asked, confused. He smirked, going to his bag on the stage. From it, he pulled a bottle of wine.

"Booze, my dear, is the solution to all the world's problems."

"Classy," I said, getting up. Around other people, I would have to control my sarcasm, but I felt Liam always knew when I was being funny and not being hurtful. Liam smiled, taking a mock bow.

"Do you want some? Or perhaps?" He reached into his bag, pulling out a bottle of water. I took the water, unscrewing the cap. "A toast. To the magic of theater," he said, and I grinned, clinking my bottle against his.

"The magic of theater," I said, and we drank.

We rehearsed until 10pm, although as it got later, it mostly became conversation and giggling, exactly what I needed after a horrid day. Liam went through the whole bottle of wine, and by 10pm, I could see it was time for me to go.

"Shall I call someone for you?" I asked, as we finished the scene. "I really should get to bed."

"Like the Phantom of the Opera, I can make my way to my cave through the bowels of the theater," he said, reaching out to kiss my hand.

"Ok then. As long as you don't go strangling people with nooses or obsessing over chorus girls." I didn't draw back as quickly as I should have.

"Chorus girls can be very enticing," he whispered, meeting my eyes. I stood rigid, fighting hard against giving into the feelings that I knew we both shared. The warmth was back, the sparkle, and I knew it. "Thank you, my dear," he said. "Not all would put up with what you have put up with."

"I didn't," I reminded him softly, meeting his eyes. "I ran away, remember?"

"I do," he whispered. The pain tracing his eyes made me look away. But as I did, I suddenly noticed a pale face at the door of the theater. I screamed and my muscles froze. Liam grabbed my arm, startled, and half pulled me behind him as he looked in the direction I was staring at. He laughed then, heading to the switchboard to push the button to open the theater.

"It's only Porsche," he said, laughing as he let her in. "Porsche, my beloved Russian import, what can we do for you?"

She looked tired, her backpack over-stuffed as she strode down the aisle to the theater, waving a paper at Liam.

"I've just checked the ticket list for opening night, your night. We've sold out."

My jaw dropped and I clapped my hands like a child. "Oh my God, that's amazing."

"Wait." Liam waved his hand in my direction to silence me. "Why do you look unhappy, then?"

"Because an anonymous benefactor bought up every ticket we had left, and donated them to the leukemia treatment center, as well as the center of blood diseases."

"So...isn't that exactly what we wanted?" I looked from one to the other, confused. Porsche shook her head.

"The tickets were purchased from France, and signed 'S'."

"Selene," Liam growled and I perked up, suddenly remembering the woman I met in the hallway. From the dark look on Liam's face, his origin story came back to me. The beautiful dark French woman in the club who had cursed him.

"She's here," I blurted out and they both turned to me, shocked.

"What?"

"She's here. I met her, in the hallway, a few days ago. She was looking for you, Liam ... I'm sorry, I didn't make the connection at all. But she fits your description."

Liam hissed, baring his fangs, and I took a step back. Porsche took the steps two at a time, immediately grabbing his arm. In seconds, I was amazed to see his fangs recede and his face start to gain color again.

"Whoa," I breathed, staring at him as the dark circles receded and he began to look human again. "That's what Shields do."

Porsche gave me a tight-lipped smile.

"Among other things. We'll go to a supernatural party sometime and I'll show you. Liam?"

"Have you seen her since?" he asked, turning to me and at once seeming sober, his eyes focusing on my face.

"No..."

"You think she knows?" Porsche asked.

Liam shrugged. "I don't know. Amy, Shannon offered you residence, right? All of her performers get put up in a hotel if they need."

"Yeah, but I live here," I said.

Liam shook his head. "I'll tell her you need to stay there to focus. She'll love it."

"You think I'm in danger?" I asked and Liam took a step forward, taking my hand. The three of us made a strange chain of support.

"I think I want to be extra cautious. This is my mess, not yours." Even though the words were not meant maliciously, they stung. He was reminding me that I ran when he needed me. I felt horrible, my chest aching with despair. Liam had been nothing but supportive to me, and now, he was taking care of my safety before even his own. "You stay in the hotel until we figure out what this bitch wants. Porsche..."

"I'm staying with you," she said, and he gave her a look, but said nothing.

"Amy, I want you to go straight to your room and pack whatever you need for the next week. The school has been on lockdown for four hours and it's dark, so she can't wander unnoticed. She would never do anything that sloppy. Go now, and I'll be there shortly, after I call Shannon."

"But...." I started, and he waved his hand.

"Go. Please, Amy."

His eyes pleaded with me and I nodded, grabbing my bag and hurrying out of the theater. My heart was hammering as hard as this morning, but I realized one thing: I trusted Liam.

CHAPTER 18: LIAM

As soon as Amy left, I turned to Porsche, who had already begun to talk, "Do you think she's just hanging out again, or she's jealous? If she knows about you and Amy, then..."

"She's probably just checking in," I replied, moving away. As soon as I did, I felt the pain of transformation return. "Listen, Porsche, you should go too."

"No," she replied, crossing her arms. "I've been here every other time, why would I disappear now?"

"Because it was ... different before." I gritted my teeth as I felt my heart stop pounding. After all these years, it was still a shock. "You're not as strong as before, Porsche."

"And you know as well as I do that a Shield's power increases as their human body fails," she replied. "We really are an idiotic creation."

"Porsche..." I sighed. "If something happens and I'm not nearby..." I took a step closer to her. "Maybe we should just do it now."

"No." She shook her head. "Not yet, Liam. I still have some life left in me. I don't need you."

"Yet," I said, with a soft smile.

"Yet," she agreed. "But Amy does. And I could be blind, mute and dumb and still see that there is something happening between you two again. Call Shannon. I'll compromise with you. I spend all day at rehearsal anyway, and all night with you. I'll do double duty and keep you both safe."

"Thank you," I said, careful not to touch her. If Selene was looking for a fight, I didn't want to lose my vampire form.

"Anytime." She grinned. "Now, go get her and I'll take her over. Selene won't be able to find her if I take her."

"Even if she does, she'll be repulsed by the smell of you two," I replied, and Porsche lightly punched my shoulder.

"Go."

xxxxxxxxxxxxxxxx

The phone call was quick. Shannon rolled her eyes so loudly I could hear it and told me where the performers were staying.

I snuck down the corridors, careful to stay in the shadows, and knocked on Amy's door. It opened immediately, and she stood there, bag in hand and ready to go.

"What about my dad?" she asked, and I winced.

"It's best no one knows," I said. "Listen, Porsche is going to be your escort all day, ok? One of the effects of a Shield is that a vampire can't track you if you are touching her."

"That's why you two are so touchy," Amy said. "Whenever I saw you two together...she was always touching you."

"Invisibility cloak," I said, taking Amy's hand and leading her down the hallway after she locked her door. "At their most powerful, they can shield a whole theater just by sitting there. Reduce everything in it to human."

"When?" she asked and I looked down.

"What?"

"When are they at their most powerful?"

I swallowed, looking both ways before going down another hallway. I was trying to pick the least populated corridors.

"When they are dying. That's why chronically ill Shields are great, they are always powerful. They gain the most power at the minute of their death both to protect their masters and, after death, to have the power transferred to the next in the bloodline. They are a stupid creation," I echoed Porsche's words. "So powerful and yet wiped out in one stumble."

"Are you her master?" Amy asked, flatly, and I shook my head.

"Deals like the one Porsche made with me are usually for a life of service...but we never made any oath or anything. It's just an understanding."

"Liam," Amy said, stopping suddenly. "You aren't going to do that to me, are you?"

"What?" I asked. We were almost to the front entrance and I didn't want to stop.

"If something happens to me...change me..."

"Amy," I turned to her, shocked. "I would never do this to anyone who didn't wish it. I would never go against your wishes."

"Because...I mean...I'm sick too," she whispered and I cupped her face in my hands, drawing her close. To her credit, she didn't flinch.

"Not unless you asked, Amy. I will never hurt you."

She bit her lip, nodding, and we stayed a moment like that; looking into each other's eyes. Finally, she broke away.

"There's Porsche."

"Right." I pulled her closer, and then without thinking, kissed her. She, to my surprise, kissed back. "Be safe, Amy."

She nodded, finally breaking my grasp to go to Porsche. The dancer nodded to me.

"I'll take care of her. It'll be fine tomorrow. You'll see."

"Sure. I'll see you at rehearsal," I said, even though I wasn't sure I quite believed myself. "Go."

Watching the two women in my life walk away into the night was probably one of the hardest things I had ever done. With a deep breath, I turned back to the school, which was powered down for the night. I went back down the hallway to face the darkness on my own. After all, this was my battle.

I ducked into my office, locked the door and opened a bottle of gin. It was going to be a long night and I might as well have some company.

CHAPTER 19: AMY

Porsche pulled me along the sidewalk to the hotel at an alarming rate, chattering away as if we had just left a party.

"It'll be ok, Amy, really, you'll see. It'll help for when you graduate. You can't live at the school forever."

I nodded, trying to make sense of what she was saying.

"Do you live in a hotel in Russia?"

"Ballet dormitories, fully furnished," she replied, with a shrug. "And fully serviced. Very luxurious."

"Right," I said, looking over my shoulder as the school got smaller and smaller. "Do you think Liam will be alright?"

"He's just over-reacting," she said. "Really, Selene is just annoying. She doesn't usually fight. Now, do you have everything?"

"I forgot my AZT," I said, suddenly, patting my pockets. I turned, but Porsche pulled me back.

"I have some. Wow, bonding," she said. "You can borrow. Now, let's go."

"Don't you need it?" I asked, and Porsche winced, shaking her head.

"Nope. Let's go."

The hotel that the performers were staying at was lovely—far better than anything I had ever stayed at with my father on our rare family vacations. Porsche checked me in, and led me toward the elevator, all without letting go of my hand.

"They probably think we're lovers, checking in for a night of passion," I joked, trying to keep the mood light.

She eyed me. "Wouldn't be the first time."

"Oh." I said and then stopped, realizing what she was telling me. "*OH.*"

"Is that a problem?" she asked, and I shook my head.

"No, of course not. I just thought ... you ... and men ... men stare at you all the time."

"Either works for me," she said, leading me out of the elevator. "Although it's not a well-known fact."

"I won't tell anyone! Wow, Porsche, you're the most interesting person I know," I blurted out as we reached my room. She laughed.

"You're dating a vampire," she pointed out.

"Dated. Past tense," I countered as I stepped into the room.

"You sure about that?" She asked, raising an eyebrow. "Good night, Amy. Sleep well."

"You're not staying?" I asked, shocked.

She shook her head. "Double duty. Back to school to deal with your undead headmaster. Slash Boyfriend. Slash Vampire." She handed over her pill bottle and then, nodding, she closed the door. I was alone in the room, with only distant voices coming from another room to keep me company.

I wasn't going to cry, not this time. Porsche was right. This would be good for me, and good for Liam and me to not be so close together. I had to leave school sometime, and what better time to do it than during my first professional production?

I got ready for bed, popping the pills she had given me. Out of curiosity, I looked at the label.

"Porsche Caroline De Ritter" it read. So Porsche was her real name and not just a cheesy dance name. The dosage was the same as mine. We could practically be pill buddies. What surprised me was the date.

Prescribed: September 2012.
Refills: 0.

This was only a 3 month supply. So either she had switched doctors, prescriptions...or the more likely option: she was done. Porsche was no longer in HIV positive status. She was in full blown AIDS and they weren't working anymore.

I sat down, staring at the bottle. Knowing that meant so many things to me. She had immortality, I did not. Her transformation would change our status.

To my surprise, tears sprung to my eyes. Vampire or not, the first real friend I made here, who understood, was going to die a lot sooner than I was. And I'd be alone. Alive and alone.

Hot tears poured down my face. I didn't have any memories of my mother, only feelings of warmth and comfort and safety. I had seen pictures and they were like looking into a crystal ball and seeing my future. No matter whether it was 10, 20, or 30 years down the line, it was coming.

I curled under the blankets, my tears staining the pillow. My head began to pound, and I closed my eyes. This was a nightmare; all of this was a nightmare that I never wanted to wake up from.

But it was reality, and it was mine.

I waited for sleep to take me as a million thoughts ran through my head. But it never came. I drifted into a doze around dawn, although I was wide awake when the alarm went off.

Sitting up, I went to turn it off when the phone rang.

"Hello?" I said groggily.

"Are you ok?" came the voice on the other end.

"Liam?" I asked. "Yes, I'm fine. Are you ok?"

"Yes," he said. There was an awkward silence. "I'll see you at 1pm today."

"Ok," I said and he hung up without another word. Just then, there was a tap on the door.

"Geez, sensory overload," I mumbled, as I struggled out of bed and pulled my hair into a bun, before pulling it open. I realized I should have looked before I did that. However, it was just a room-service man standing there with a tray.

"Breakfast," he said, and I shook my head.

"I didn't order anything?"

"You're one of those actors, right?" he asked.

"Yes, but..."

"Charged to the production company then."

"Right. Uh...put it over there please," I said, and he wheeled the tray in. I signed the bill, writing in a tip to make up for my cluelessness.

Lifting the silver lid, I was greeted with a platter of fresh strawberries and hot muffins. Grinning, I dug in. I could certainly get used to this.

It turned out that breakfast became the highlight of every morning. I would arrive at rehearsal fortified by breakfast only to be screamed at by Shannon for every move I made. It got to the point where I was second-guessing things I knew, like stage right and stage left.

I felt overwhelmed at the end of every night, my head hitting the pillow with a thud. The professional performers had a lot more contacts and experience than anyone at school did, and I was way out of my league. I thought I knew everyone in the industry; Sarah and I read the trade papers obsessively. But here they were, discussing people I had never heard of, and rolling their eyes when I asked a question.

"For any chorus members." Shannon stood up one day, clearing her throat and getting our attention. "There's a friend of mine who's casting for teenage-looking girls at Torrid Night Club at 2pm today for a commercial. The shoot doesn't conflict with chorus rehearsal, so you're welcome to try your luck. I make no recommendations for anyone." Her eyes landed on me, and I knew she was basically telling me I had no shot. However, I also knew that I should take every opportunity I could, and so I made a mental note to see if I could sneak down there today, if Liam would let me. Today was only a lightening rehearsal anyway, one of the many as the show drew closer. "Demo reels can be brought in as well."

I bit my lip at that. I barely knew what a demo reel was and I was fairly certain that I didn't have one. But I had to try, at the very least.

As soon as rehearsal was over, I called Liam's direct line to ask him what I should do. But instead of his voice, his secretary answered.

"Hello?"

"Hi, it's, uh ... Amy. Can I speak to Liam, please?"

"He's got student meetings all afternoon, Amy. But if you can come by..."

"No, I can't come by." It was already 1pm.

"Oh. Can I take a message then?"

"Just..." My mouth went dry, unsure of what to say. If I had been at school, this would be easy. I could just pop my head in and ask him. But now, we were a few miles apart and I felt like I needed his support. For the first time since this whole mess started, I couldn't get it. "Just tell him I'll be late for rehearsal, and if it's an issue, he can call me on my cell."

"Will do," she said, and I could hear her scribbling down the message. "Anything else?"

"Maybe he can call me regardless, ASAP?" I said, cursing myself for sounding so weak.

"I'll do my best, Amy," she said, and hung up, leaving me alone again.

I went up to the hotel room to get my headshot and resume and then headed back down. I could walk to the nightclub, no problem, but I still hurried. I had no idea what a commercial audition entailed. If they handed me a script, then that was no problem, I knew how to act. But this wasn't theater, so was it different? Who was I supposed to ask for? What was I supposed to do?

I was the first one there, when I got there. Luckily, someone at the front directed me to the right room, and someone else showed me where to sign in. It asked for an agency or recommendation. Remembering Shannon's words, I left it blank. I thought about putting down Liam's name or the Academy, but decided not to, at the last minute. I was here on my own, after all.

Someone else came out, and handed me a script, which made me breathe a sigh of relief. It was a commercial for a funeral home, which left a heavy feeling in my chest. How long before I saw one of those for real?

I was escorted in after only a few minutes in the waiting room. Unlike the Gatsby audition, this room was small, probably used as a changing room when the club was opened. There was just one person in it, a cameraman, who nodded to me and clicked the camera on, making the red light flash.

"All right, take your mark," he said. I looked around, confused, until I saw a masking tape "x" on the floor. Thankful I figured that out, I slid over to it, rooting my feet firmly on it.

"Great. So just slate and then I'll read for you," he said.

"Slate?" I asked, confused. He rolled his eyes.

"Name, agency contact."

"Oh...I don't have an agency."

"Just your phone number, then." He looked bored. I stuttered through the sentence and he nodded.

"All right. Now, look at the camera when you say your lines and don't move from your mark."

"Don't move?" I looked down at the spot and looked back up, confused. How was I supposed to portray character if I didn't move?

"That's right. Don't move."

I saw the red light click off and then on again, and I looked at the script in my hands one last time.

"And ... action."

The scene itself was easy enough. I had long since learned how to cry on cue, and I made sure to use that skill. The lines flowed naturally, but I felt restricted and stiff by my lack of movement. Twice, I bobbed out of frame and had to be waved back in. The tears that flowed down my face felt forced, and I had never been so happy to reach the end of a scene.

"Ok, thanks," he said, looking right at me.

I realized I was done and nodded. "Uh...so..." I said, unsure. The cameraman rolled his eyes.

"They'll call you if they are interested."

"Ok," I replied. I knew I had done something wrong, and I felt my cheeks burning as I left the room. Everything about that audition had been different. I had never had a camera in my face like that before, and I had never been so restricted to one spot.

Even though I was supposed to be at rehearsal and seeing him in less than an hour, I couldn't help but text Liam. I had to know what I did wrong.

Are you busy? Can you call me for a quick second? I wrote, checking it for spelling before sending it. I had barely taken 3 steps before my phone rang.

"Hello?" I asked, knowing it was him.

"I got your message," he said, talking softly. I assumed he was already in the theater. "What's the matter?"

"Nothing. I'm sorry I'm going to be late, but Shannon told me about a commercial audition, so I thought I'd go."

"As you said," he said, approvingly. "You should always take opportunities like that, especially when your schedule can be re-arranged with little inconvenience. We're just working on some fight choreography, so you'd be sitting here doing nothing anyway."

"Yeah," I replied, my voice sounding far off. Liam picked up on it and made a noise of concern.

"How'd it go?"

"Uh...the acting part went ok," I said, as I walked down the sidewalk, falling into a rhythm. "The words poured out of my mouth. But the rest of it was weird. It was a little room with only one guy on the panel, filming, and he told me to 'slate', which I had no idea about, and then he made me stay on this little 'X' the whole time, and not have freedom of character movement. Do you think it was sketchy?"

Liam laughed at that, although it was friendly.

"That's film and TV auditions for you, Amy. Always exactly like that. They are very different from theater, and it's almost as if it's a whole different world. Film and theater actors sometimes don't translate over. But you felt ok when it came down to the actual acting part, yes?"

"Yes." I nodded, even though he couldn't see me. "I just..." I closed my eyes for a moment. "I wish that I could have talked to you beforehand. I felt like an idiot. In fact..." I took a deep breath, knowing what I was about to say was powerful. "I think talking to you before the Gatsby audition was the only thing that kept me sane."

There was a silence on the other end of the phone, but it felt comfortable. Now that I was talking to Liam, the panic of the audition had gone away and I felt fine. I hadn't realized how much I needed him, and needed his advice and support, until this very moment. Yes, I could act, and that came easy, but he was right, it came down to so much more than just acting. I thought I had been ready for all this, but it was clearly going to be harder than I thought.

"Anytime, Amy," he said, and I could hear the noise behind him increase. "I have to go. I'll see you soon, though?" It was more than just a confirmation, he sounded hopeful.

"Yes," I said. "About 20 minutes. 30 if you are feeling generous and want to give me time to stuff my face."

He chuckled at that.

"Make it forty. I'll see you then." He hung up quickly, and I put my phone into my pocket, continuing to walk down the sidewalk, and feeling more alone. The sun was shining, and the birds were chirping and I could hear children playing in a nearby park. The dark mood over me had lifted, and I felt a lot better. I had just finished one rehearsal, I had an audition and now I was headed to rehearsal for a spot I had won over hundreds of hopefuls. Life wasn't so bad.

Although I didn't want to admit it, I knew part of my mood was due to the fact that I was going to see Liam in a matter of minutes.

I felt that painful feeling in my chest again as I realized how little time I had left at the school. In a matter of weeks, I would be permanently moved out and in the world on my own. Gatsby would soon be on tour, and there would be no coming back to the school after that, no safe haven to look forward to. I had never gone more than two days without seeing my dad in my entire life, and soon I would be going months. And after Gatsby, who knew? If I didn't make it here, there were other cities, other theaters, other tours. It was a scary thought, and it didn't seem real that my entire world was about to change.

<u>CHAPTER 20: LIAM</u>

I realized when she walked in, I'd been watching the door for her the entire time. My head had been pounding all morning, and I was exhausted from last night's excursions. If we didn't only have a few days of rehearsal left, I would have already called it for today. I wanted a hair of the dog, enough water to drown a horse, and a nap that took fifteen hours. Unfortunately, those things had only been possible when I was a human movie star. Now, as a vampire headmaster, I supposed people expected me to be somewhat responsible. Still, I knew I hadn't been as involved today as I should have been.

As soon as she walked in, I felt my heart beat speed up and I couldn't help but smile. She was here, and I could relax.

"Let's take five minutes," I called to the fight choreographers on stage. The boys stopped, panting, and headed off for their water bottles. I motioned to Amy to join me back stage. "How are you?"

"Better now that I'm here," she said, looking around. "No, uh … unexpected visitors?"

"No, nothing." I shook my head, watching her. Her hair was pulled up, but a few strands were falling into her fresh face. She looked beautiful and young, and I knew her future held nothing but promise and hope. "Porsche and I patrolled most of the night, but nothing came up. Selene is like that. She'll show up long enough to scare me, but she has yet to do any harm. I suspect she's just checking in to make sure I keep my promise."

"Your promise?" Amy asked, reaching into her backpack as we talked.

"Why she turned me," I said, keeping my voice down. "With such a public persona, I was guaranteed to keep the secret unless I wanted to ruin my life. Supposedly, I had it all. Vampires could always find me for help, I have a truck ton of money and contacts, but I also will make sure to keep it secret unless I want to ruin my own life. I was the perfect candidate. Hell, I should have predicted it would happen to me."

"Liam," she said, compassionately and I looked down to find her holding a container. "Do you want a cookie?"

I laughed, nodding. "Yes," I said, taking one of her father's secret recipe cookies. They were so loaded with chocolate it was a wonder they had any other ingredients. I had them once or twice before and they never failed to make me feel better. At the moment, however, it was Amy's smile that was assisting in that endeavor.

We locked eyes for a moment, and the intensity of the gaze was so fierce it almost overwhelmed me. I tilted my head down a fraction of an inch, and she responded, arching her neck upwards. Our lips were only inches apart when we were interrupted by a string of swear words.

"What the..." I pulled away the curtain. On the other end of the stage, Deon was standing there, his phone in one hand, his face the very picture of stunned. I didn't even have to ask to know what the problem was, I recognized the look immediately. He wasn't sad, or upset, or grieving. He wasn't in pain or angry. That was the look of an actor who was simultaneously happy he got a part and stunned because he had a conflict. "Deon?" I asked, as Amy came to stand beside me. He turned his head toward me, waving his phone.

"I...the TV role...full time, Paris...Friday... 3 months, with extension."

It would have taken a normal person half a day to figure out what he was saying, but I understood immediately. "You can't do the show then," I said, calmly. Deon had yet to change the expression on his face.

"Yes...no...But I...What should I...oh man." He seemed so overwhelmed he could barely get the sentence out. Everyone was gathering around him in excitement, but his gaze was locked with mine. I forced a smile onto my face as I stepped forward. Deon came over at once, looking much younger than his 18 years.

"Liam?" he said, unsure and I nodded.

"This is what I wanted for you guys, your whole lives. Why are you looking so unsure?" I asked. "Deon, you've been here for years, and you've been trained since you could speak to do this. Every day of school, every exercise and workshop was so you could be prepared for this day, this moment in your life."

"But the show..." he said, and I put my hand on his shoulder. Amy stood beside me, and I couldn't look at her. The most talent in the entire school was now within two feet of me and I was about to lose both of them.

"Don't worry about the show. You're ready for this. For all of this."

He nodded, although I could see the fear in his eyes.

"Amy," he said, turning to her. "I'm sorry..."

"Don't be sorry," she replied, reaching up to hug him. "Don't be. I almost did the same thing, remember? We'll work together again, I'm sure."

"You're going to make it big, girl." He hugged her tight, and then turned to me. "I guess I should..."

"Pack," I said, nodding. "And go see Peter; he'll be happy for you."

184

"Right. Yes," he said, a grin spreading across his face. "Thank you, Liam. For everything."

"You won't say that when your set call is at 4am," I blurted out, and he laughed.

After hugs all around, Deon picked up his stuff, and headed out the door, standing two inches taller than when he walked in. There was a silence that fell over the cast then.

"Well," I said, turning to Amy. "I guess it's you and me."

Her jaw fell open. "Every show? ... I'm glad," she said, quietly, her hand brushing mine. "I'd rather do it with you. With you, it feels like it's just... a conversation. "

"I'm glad I get a second chance to do this with you," I replied, and she met my eyes, seeing my meaning as clear as day. She looked away, and I turned to the cast. They were still shell shocked.

"Right. Everyone forget Deon's blocking, right now. Forget it, erase it from your memories, it's gone. We need to be happy for him, but we need to focus on our show now. From now on, every show is with me, and I want no more interruptions for the rest of the day." I even reached into my pocket and pulled out my phone, turning it off as an example. "You have three minutes to set yourself from the top. Ready, set, go!"

I watched them scramble to their places. Amy put down her backpack, and fixed her hair, heading toward her entrance. In the chaos, her phone rang, and although I should have scolded her, I let her answer it. At the moment, I was so happy to be able to perform with her; to still have her that I couldn't have denied her anything.

"Hello? Yes? Wait, what? *What?* One second." She turned back to me, and held the phone out, confused. "It's for you."

"Now what?" I sighed, going toward her and taking the phone. I didn't recognize the number, but I assumed it was one of Shannon's people. Seems like I had turned my phone off at exactly the right time.

"Hello?" I asked, and an unfamiliar voice spoke to me.

"Is this the same Liam that is in charge of the Leopard Spot Academy?"

"Uh, yes…" I felt a bit annoyed. "Who's this?"

"And you know a Porsche De Ritter?"

"Yes?" I gripped the phone tighter, turning away. "What's happened?"

"Liam, Porsche has listed you as her emergency contact. My name is Chelsea, and I work for Norfinch Health Care. She was admitted today after a fall at work."

"Oh God." I ducked behind the curtain. "Is she ok?" I knew that sending Porsche off to her own rehearsal after being up all night was not a good idea, but she had insisted.

"It appears she has a bacterial infection. She's on IV antibiotics right now, and she's asleep, but we thought her contacts should be notified. Visiting hours are from 5 to 7pm today and she should be awake by then. Her condition is serious, but stable."

"I'll be there. Please, you can call me on this number if there's any news," I said, biting my lip with worry. "Is she…going to be ok?"

The nurse sighed, and I could hear her clicking away at her computer.

"It's an expected AIDS complication. Infections are common."

"But also serious," I said, my heart hammering in my chest. Could anything else possibly go wrong today? "Please, tell me the truth."

There was a silence on the other end of the phone, and then Chelsea spoke, "At the moment, we're hopeful she'll recover."

The words hit me like a sledgehammer. Amy was beside me, taking my hand, wrapping her arms around me as I managed to hang up the phone. Just as I had been able to guess Deon's news from years of experience, she could guess what had happened on the phone from her own years. She held me tight as I tried to get hold of my emotions.

"You can go to her," she said, softly, but I shook my head, wiping my eyes.

"No. Porsche's a theater addict, she'd kill me if I interrupted rehearsal. Visiting hours are from 5 to 7, we can go after. Will you...will you come with me?" I asked, and she nodded, reaching up to wipe a tear away from my face. I hadn't realized my eyes were leaking until then and I struggled to get it under control.

"Of course," she said, and then our lips met.

The kiss was soft, and slow, yet needed. I didn't want to break apart from her, and it seemed we were clinging onto each other out of necessity. I wanted her; I wanted her so badly that my muscles ached. More than anything, I wanted to forget the pain and get lost in the pleasure of her body. But now was not the time or place. Finally, we pulled apart, and my forehead rested on hers.

"It's ok, isn't it?" she asked. "I mean...you made a promise, to Porsche."

"I did." I nodded. "But I'll mourn the human part of her all the time. This life, Amy, this life is a curse and why she wants it is beyond me."

"To live," she whispered. "She wants to live."

I could hear Amy's own heartbeat, loud in her chest, and feel her own warm skin against mine. It nearly broke my heart; that this beautiful young girl that I had come to fall in love with wanted to live just as badly. And here I was, handed immortality and I didn't want it.

Amy's arms squeezed my torso tightly, and I held on to her for all it was worth. I wanted her, above all else, and I had to keep her safe. If I was going to be alone for all of eternity, I wanted her with me as long as I could have her.

CHAPTER 21: AMY

I was nervous before I even fully opened my eyes. My alarm hadn't gone off yet, but I knew I couldn't sleep any longer. It was much later than normal, nearly 11am. It was opening day and in a few hours, I would be on stage, beside Liam.

The last few days had been exhausting. Between Deon quitting, Gatsby rehearsal, and Porsche, I was tired. She had spent the last few days in the hospital, barely waking long enough to say hello. And I had no doubts, when she was finally released, that it wouldn't be for long.

She hadn't even wanted to be admitted, insisting it was useless. Liam had protested, and as usual, he got his way. I knew she was delaying her transformation for our safety. Liam was sure she wouldn't be a Shield after her descent into vampirism. But all of it was still hard to watch, and just added to the stress of opening night.

I had the day off from Gatsby today, so I could be prepared for tonight. At 2pm, we had a press conference at the school, for Liam and I, and then at 6, a photo shoot before the curtain went up at 8pm. I was trying to stay calm, but nothing was working. Liam had walked me through every step of the day, explaining what to do and what not to do. He reminded me to breathe, and to say nothing that I didn't want the whole world to know. There was apparently no such thing as "off the record," and I wasn't to trust any reporter, which made sense to me. But even with all of his instruction, I was still glad he was going to be beside me the whole time. Especially with the media frenzy surrounding the fact that he was going to be doing all the shows now, not just the one. The remainder of our shows had been sold out and there was a waiting list. It made me nervous and excited all at the same time.

Getting up, I headed for the shower, checking my phone on the way. There were about 50 *Good Luck* texts from my friends, and smiley faces. Last night, Dad and I had dinner at home. It was a nice break from the chaos that was surrounding me. He had told me he was proud of me, and wished me luck, which was music to my ears. I knew he thought acting was a risky career, but with Liam's help, I felt like I could fly.

Except all that would be over soon. I tried to push that thought away as I got into the shower. I vowed to enjoy this day for all it was worth, and when the time came, I would face what I needed to.

I took extra care in the shower to make sure everything was shaved, washed and clean. I scrubbed my face three times, and shampooed my hair twice, and then blow dried it with a round brush, something I had done about twice in my life. I was going to get my makeup done in the theater before the press conference, so I didn't have to worry about it.

I chose tight jeans and boots, with a tunic shirt that belted at my waist. Satisfied with my appearance in the mirror, I picked up my purse, and slipped out the door, my heart beating fast.

"Ammmmmmyyyyy." I wasn't out the door five seconds when one of my floor mates, Charisma, attacked me with a hug. "Are you excited?"

"I feel more like puking, but I hear that's excitement," I said, giving her a hug back. "What are you doing today?"

"Being your slave." She smiled at me. "Anything you need me to do?"

"Um…" I shrugged. "No. I was just going to get breakfast…or lunch… and then go to hair and makeup. We have a press conference and all."

"Exccccitting." Charisma was possibly one of the sweetest girls I had ever met. She never had an unkind word for anyone and was always genuine in her responses. "Want me to come?"

"Sure, you can be my body guard." I linked my arm in hers, heading down to the canteen. It was then that I saw Selene again, crossing the campus. She had sunglasses and a fashionable trench coat on, but I still recognized her. She carried herself in such a way that couldn't be missed, with her nose high in the air and her shoulders squared.

I froze, making Charisma stumble.

"What?" she asked, following my eye line. "Who's that?"

"No one," I said, even as I took out my phone and frantically sent a text to Liam. *Selene is on campus. I'll be in the cafe.* "Just...someone I thought I knew. Let's go."

I moved faster down the hall, practically dragging Charisma with me. We had barely grabbed food when Liam burst into the canteen, his jaw set.

"Are you alright?" he asked, and I nodded. Charisma looked from me to him and back again.

"What's going on?"

"Nothing," he said, shaking his head. "Amy just needs...I need Amy to come with me. Sorry," he apologized to her. "Last minute prep."

"No problem." She released my arm. "Break a leg tonight, guys! I have tickets for tomorrow."

"Thanks," I said, giving her a quick hug and then following Liam out into the hallway, my food long since forgotten. "Liam, it's ok. I just saw her, she didn't see me."

"I should have known." He shook his head, dragging me along the hallway to the staff quarters. "I shouldn't have been so stupid."

"What?" I asked, struggling to keep up.

"I'm sorry, Amy. I thought we were safe when she didn't show her face. But she bought all the tickets to opening night, and I should have known she would show up today. She'll be watching tonight, for sure."

"Do you think she wants to hurt me?" I asked, fear leaping into my throat. Liam shook his head.

"No. Selene is not usually the...violent type," he said. "And even if she does try, there will be truckloads of security there, to make sure we're safe."

"Uh...Did you get vampire security or something?" I asked, as he put his key in the lock.

"Sort of," he replied, ushering me into the room. I turned to give him a funny look, but when I entered the room, I saw what he meant. Sitting crossed legged on his bed, looking about four shades paler, Porsche was slowly doing her makeup.

"Porsche!" I cried, flying across the room to give her a hug.

"Hey, Amy." Her voice was soft, and she felt about ten pounds lighter, her already thin frame feeling skeletal under my arms. She was burning with heat, her face shiny with sweat and her heartbeat could be heard even by my human ears. "How are you?" I could see the lesions on her arms, and subtly, when she opened her mouth, I could see the sores. I didn't think it was possible to downward spiral as fast as she did and I wondered how long she had been hiding it from me, and from Liam. He seemed just as shocked as I was to see her this way.

192

"Forget me, how are you?" I asked. Porsche's eyes went above my head, to meet Liam's, who sighed.

"It's better that she's here, Amy. For you ... and for her. So that she's closer to me if anything happens."

"And for him," she said, with a soft smile. "My power grows every hour. By tonight, neither Liam nor Selene will transform."

"But that means..." I said, trailing off with horror. She shrugged.

"Doesn't matter anymore, Amy. It'll all be over soon. But tonight, don't worry about me. Worry about you."

"It shouldn't happen this quickly," I said, looking up at her. "I mean, you've only been off AZT a few months."

"I'm refusing treatment," she said, putting down her mascara brush. She looked skeletal, her eyes cloudy and her cheeks hollow. "I'm done with all this."

"So why not now?" I asked, looking to Liam. He shrugged.

"Porsche's stubborn. She wants to protect us first. So we'll wait as long as she can hold out...the run of the show at least." Although he was speaking the words, I believed he disagreed with it as much as I did. His face was stony, and his eyes were dark.

"Thank you," I said, turning back to her. She smiled, her eyes a bit teary.

"Anytime," she said. "I hope we can still be friends when I'm on the other side, Amy."

"Of course," I replied. "It's much more taboo for you to back an actor with no experience than for me to be friends with a vampire."

Porsche laughed at that, leaning back against the pillows. "This is indeed true."

Liam shook his head, going to the mini fridge to get us both a bottle of water.

"Porsche, do you feel up to doing Amy's makeup? I don't feel comfortable letting her onto the theater right now."

"Would you?" I turned back to her. "I'm about as useful with makeup as I am fighting a dragon."

"Sure, if you can be patient," she replied, glancing at her makeup supplies. "I'm a bit slow today."

I settled down on the bed beside her. It was hard to look; to see my future staring me in the face and know it waited for me each day. I hoped, when the day came, I would be at peace with it.

By 1:30pm, my hair was teased into millions of little curls that sat high on my head, and my makeup made me look like a supermodel. Although it took her a few hours, Porsche made me look more beautiful than I had ever looked in my life.

"Wow," I said as I looked in the handheld mirror. "Thank you."

"Just enhancing what is already there, darling," she said, as Liam came out of the bathroom, fully dressed. "What do you think?" she asked him.

Liam didn't say anything for a moment. His eyes twinkled as they traveled from my neck to my eyebrows in awe. I blushed, looking down at my nails which were painted and shaped.

"You look beautiful," he said. "But then...you always do."

"Thank you," I whispered and our eyes locked. This had been happening for days; these moments of intensity. We still hadn't talked about our almost kiss backstage. It hung in the air like an elephant in the room.

"Ok you two." Porsche slowly swung her legs around, standing up shakily. In a moment, Liam was beside her, supporting her. "I'm going to brush my teeth and change. It's almost press conference time."

"Do you want lunch?" Liam asked her. She shook her head. "Or anything? You're still human, Porsche, so I suggest some nutrition."

"Nope." She closed the bathroom door, leaving Liam and I alone. He sat down beside me, so close I could see his pulse beat in his throat. He looked gorgeous, with his hair slicked back and a thin chain hanging around his neck, peeking through the open buttons on his dark dress shirt. His cologne wafted from his neck, a familiar scent that I realized I had missed.

"Are you ready?" I asked, and he nodded, reaching one hand up to tuck a strand of hair from my face.

"I'm glad you're here, Amy," he said, and I sighed.

"Not for long though."

"The best director I ever had once gave me a piece of advice," he said, reaching down to put his hand over mine. I let him, enjoying the comfort of his touch. "We were about to go on stage, and he grabbed my arm right before the curtain went up. 'Enjoy your time in the cabin with the other characters' he said, 'for it is very short and will never return. Live in the moment.' I think that night was the best show of my life. The real world is scary, Amy, even I know that. But our time as Beauty and the Beast...that is

195

short and controlled and ends happily. And so we have to live in that moment."

His face was inches from mine and this time I didn't let the moment go to waste. I kissed him hard and fast, as if I was drowning and he was my life line. I put my hands on the back of his head, pressing my body closer. Liam sunk back into the pillows, pulling me on top of him, and groaned as I pressed down. Everything fit perfectly and felt so right; the feel of his body against mine, his touch, his caress.

He put his hands in my hair, pulling gently, and I moaned despite myself. We used to spend hours just snuggled up to each other, perfectly content in each other's physical presence and nothing more. When we broke up, I told myself I didn't miss it, but the truth was I was dying for him to touch me again.

His hands wandered down my back, and rested on my waist, pausing there as we continued to kiss. His eyes were closed and his face was relaxed from its earlier tension. I was in heaven.

"A-HEM." I had forgotten we weren't alone and turned around to see Porsche leaning against the doorpost looking amused. I jumped off Liam immediately.

"Uh...we were just..."

Liam stayed reclined on the bed, looking bemused as I struggled to fix my hair.

"It's ok, Porsche's an adult. She's fully aware of what we were doing."

"Not that I wanted to see it," she replied, a small smile on her face. "You two need to just get back together already. Seriously. It's just awkward."

Liam and I glanced at each other, and then away. I felt my cheeks grow hot and didn't know what to say. Apparently, neither did he, because he cleared his throat and changed the topic.

"Shall we go?"

"Yep." I may have leapt up a bit too fast. "Are you coming, Porsche?"

"You two actually have half an hour," she said, and I recognized a spark of the old fire in her eyes. "I've decided to get some food in the cafeteria before my empty stomach eats itself."

"Are you sure?" Liam asked, and she nodded.

"Uh huh," she said, although she looked ready to drop. "This is your day. Welcome to fame, Amy."

"I suppose tripping and falling in front of everyone will be bad?" I said, trying to lighten the mood.

"All press is good press." Porsche said, slowly grabbing her coat, even though it was a warm day. "It didn't hurt Liam when he was falling down drunk every night and showing up to meetings stoned."

"Uh..." Liam replied. "It kind of attracted a vampire to me?"

"Well, that's your opinion." She shrugged, and I laughed. And then she headed out the door, leaving us alone once again.

"So where were we?" Liam asked, and I looked back at him.

"Uh..." I replied, suddenly awkward. He pulled me back, so I was lying on top of him, our faces inches apart as I looked down at him. "We were...here."

"Yes, we were," he said, stroking my face.

We kissed and I felt my whole body light up with passion. I squirmed against him and he groaned, pulling me closer. I felt his need through his jeans, and could no longer deny my own.

"Liam..." I stopped suddenly.

"What?" He was breathless, looking at me as if I'd just stopped the world from spinning.

"I...you...protection?" I managed, and he shook his head, drawing me close again.

"Don't worry about it. We don't need it. Trust me. For either reasons."

"I bet there are thousands of girls whose boyfriends have told them that," I said, as his hands slid down my thighs.

"I doubt they were vampires."

"I've never..." I said, and he stopped, looking at me.

"Never?"

"Hard when you are under house arrest your whole life. And also when...unless somebody else is infected...or you really hate them..."

"No more, Amy." He put a finger to my lips, silencing me. "If you want this to be your first time ... or if you want to wait?"

"No." I shook my head. "I want you, Liam." After that, no more words were spoken. I surrendered completely to Liam's touch as I lost myself to him.

CHAPTER 22: AMY

It was only once we were walking down the hallway to the school's media room that I realized once again how nervous I was. I gripped Liam's hand tightly, feeling closer to him than ever before.

"There's no going back from this, is there?" I asked Liam, as we stood outside the door, where I could hear the press was already gathered.

"Sure there is," he said. "This industry is cruel, they will forget you in an instant if they want to."

"I don't think that's helpful," Porsche said, listening at the door. Liam shrugged, but gave me a small smile, reaching down to take my hand. He squeezed and I squeezed back, grateful. "I think they are ready for you. I'll go do your introduction. That way, if Selene is waiting for you, I'll know."

"Ok." Liam nodded, and Porsche slipped through the door, holding her head high. Liam and I stood in the hallway, in silence a moment, listening to the muffled sounds behind the door.

"Thank you," I said, looking up at him. "For all of this. For everything. I never would have been able to do any of this without you."

"Amy," he said, looking down at me. "You were meant for this. There is no way your talent wouldn't have been discovered. With or without me, you would have been an actress."

"But without you...I wouldn't have ever known how wonderful this is," I said, leaning into his side. He put his arm around me, and I closed my eyes, relaxing into his grip.

"I was ready to give up hope before I met you," he muttered, and I froze, looking up at him. He kissed the top of my head, indicating the door. "Ready?"

"Yeah." I nodded, taking a deep breath and steeling myself. Liam gave me one last hug and then opened the door.

"Ladies, and gentleman, it is with great pleasure that I introduce to you the stars of Beauty and The Beast tonight…"

Porsche was standing at the microphone, looking miles better than she did standing in the hallway. I admired her for it—it was the mark of a great performer. The rest of the introduction was drowned out by cheering and clapping. Cameras flashed and questions were being slammed at us. Liam had to drag me up on the stage; I was so blinded by the flashes.

Luckily, Liam knew how to handle the questions. He waited until people stopped screaming and then took the questions one at a time, only fielding the easiest ones to me, such as "are you happy to be a part of this show?" It was over in a flash, and before I knew it, we were heading off the stage, away from the press. I couldn't believe that they were actually so interested in me. Apart from questions about the show, they had wanted to know about my life. Where I had grown up, how I came to audition, what my hopes and dreams were. And of course, everything about my personal life, which I already chose not to answer. When they asked if I had a boyfriend, I looked away and shook my head. I could feel Liam's eyes burning at me, but I knew it was the right thing to say. If I wasn't certain of what was happening right now, the press didn't have the right to know.

The photo shoot went the same way; a constant flash of cameras, and what seemed like hundreds of paparazzi standing before us. When it was finally over, I felt out of breath, waving goodbye before heading behind the curtain. We were running late, and Liam had told me as soon as we were done, it was time to start getting ready. I had to be completely fresh-faced and re-done as Beauty, so it would take plenty of time.

I thought I was nervous for the press conference, but the nerves that descended on me as I sat in the hair and makeup chair were now worse than ever.

"Break a leg for me, darling." Porsche stuck her head through the door, looking about as bad as I felt. Still, she had a smile on her face as she came over to give me a hug. She was burning up. I could feel it from half a foot away. But I said nothing and gave her a tight hug.

"I'll be in the audience. It's past sunset and Liam hasn't changed," she whispered in my ear. I nodded, wrapping my arms around her.

"Thank you," I replied, and she gave me a quick kiss on the forehead, rubbing my shoulders.

The makeup artist finished my final coat of lip-gloss, and leaned back, nodding.

"All right, Amy, you're ready," she said. "I'll do a touch up at intermission. But you're perfect. You look just like Belle in the Disney movie."

"She was a cartoon," I said, and the makeup artist laughed, gathering up some of her stuff.

"Good luck," she said, and then she left, and I was alone for the first time in hours.

I took a deep breath, looking into the mirror. I did look like Belle, with my hair tied back and the peasant girl dress. My eyes looked huge and my skin was glowing.

Trying not to tremble, I stood up and walked out of the room. Despite not being on for a few scenes, Liam was already standing in the wings, waiting for the lights to dim.

Seeing him immediately calmed me down. My palms stopped sweating, my heart slowed and I could breathe normally again. A wave of relief washed over me and I knew I could tackle whatever was waiting for me on the stage. It was then that I realized I couldn't do this—I couldn't walk away. I may know how to act, and I may have blown Liam away at the auditions, and Shannon, but without his guidance and help, I would never be able to continue. Acting really was only half of this industry, and the rest I still had to learn.

"Hey." Liam turned around, smiling at me as he glanced at the backstage clock. "Look at you."

"Look at you. All...human still," I said, knowing that could have a double meaning, without his beast costume.

He smiled. "The power of Porsche," he replied, putting an arm around me. "You ready?"

"Yeah," I said, taking a deep breath. "Have you processed my graduation papers yet?"

He gave me a strange look, but shook his head.

"No, I didn't have time. But it's on the 22nd of June. You planning ahead?"

"Yes." I nodded, giving him a smile. "I thought...Liam, I thought I could stay. Another year. With you." I looked up to meet his eyes, taking his hand. "If that's ok."

"Amy..." he breathed, turning fully to face me. He was quiet for a few moments. "Amy, you are so beautiful...and you are so

202

talented...you are miles ahead of everyone here, and you *are* ready for this."

"No." I shook my head. "And I know it. If I stay out there with Shannon, it'll break me. I'll finish touring Gatsby, but then I want another year here. I...I need you." I said. He bit his lip, and I was surprised to see tears building in his eyes.

"I need you too, Amy," he said, and he kissed me. I wrapped my arms around him, standing on my tiptoes to not have him strain so much. There was nothing holding us back any longer. I let go of everything I was feeling, giving myself completely over to him. I had never felt so sure of anything in my life. Everything felt right.

"And if I stayed..." I said, breaking apart from him. "Got a second chance...perhaps you and I could also have a second chance?"

He smiled, nodding. "I'd like that."

"Good," I said, giving him another little nip on the lips. His smile turned devilish, and he leaned down, about to return it when a stagehand approached.

"Curtain in one minute, guys."

"Right." Liam straightened up. "Here we go."

I closed my eyes, turning to face the stage. I saw the lights dim and the opening number started to play.

"No going back now," I muttered, and Liam laid a light kiss on my head.

"Go on, Beauty. It's your time to shine," he said. I took a deep breath, looking up at his face. And then, knowing that he was behind me, I stepped forward. It was time.

As soon as I stepped out onto the stage, I didn't feel like me anymore. All of these fears had run through my head. I had worried about the silliest things; from forgetting my lines to tripping or puking on the stage. But from the second Beauty's first lines came out of my mouth, I was a different person. I was her, from head to toe. And when Liam entered the stage for the first time, I didn't see Liam, the love of my life, the vampire, my headmaster. I saw the Prince; the Beast; the hated man in the castle who intrigued and interested me like no other.

The townspeople were transformed from my classmates to people I had grown up with all my life. Ryan, who played one of my potential suitors and was actually one the nicest boys in senior year, made bile rise in my throat the second he approached me on stage. I was so distracted by Beauty's feelings and thoughts that I felt shell-shocked when intermission came and the curtain came down.

I was still in a daze when I made it off the stage. Everyone was rushing about, trying to reset the stage for the bigger scenes, which took place in the second half.

I was standing by the call sheet, trying to remember how much time I had to get changed, when someone grabbed my arm. I turned around, and Porsche nearly stumbled into me.

"What's the matter?" I asked, alarmed. She was pale as a sheet, and her jaw was clenched in a familiar way, trying to ward off nausea. "Porsche?"

"It's her," she whispered, urgently. "She's here. She's in the audience. And she obviously knows there's a Shield here, because she looks damned confused why she hasn't transformed yet."

"Oh God," I groaned, looking around as if I expected Selene to just appear.

"Where's Liam?" Porsche asked.

"He uh…he'll be getting his makeup retouched. I'll find him, all right? You just…" I looked around for a chair but she shook her head.

"I'm going back out. It'll be more effective the closer I am to her. Find Liam and tell him she's here. But she hasn't tried anything yet, so I doubt she's going to. Just…be careful out there, Amy."

"Right." I nodded, my frantic heart beat returning. "Be careful too, Porsche."

She swayed alarmingly, gripping the wall and I was hesitant to let her go.

"And Amy…" she blurted out, right before she shooed me off. "Tell Liam that it'll be tonight. For him and I."

I stood, open mouthed, but nodded, watching as she stumbled off. Tonight. Everything came down to tonight.

CHAPTER 23: AMY

When the second act started, I felt like my heart was in my throat. Everything was happening at once and it was out of my control. The media had practically attempted to break in during intermission, all too desperate to get shots of Liam again. Luckily, our security was good and held them back. However, it reconfirmed that I had made the right choice. I wasn't ready for the world out there, not yet. If anything, I wanted to spend eternity curled up in my dorm room, going to the safety of classes and snuggling with Liam in the afternoons.

"I haven't experienced night as a human like this in three years," Liam said to me, as we waited in the wings for our final cue. His arms were around my waist, and he was warm, his chest rising and falling.

"Are Shields common?" I asked, and he shook his head.

"No. After Porsche...I'll be lucky if I ever meet another one again. They really don't make themselves known, and half of them aren't ever aware of their powers. Anyway, what do you want to do next year?"

"Next year?" I turned to him and gaped.

"For a show?"

"Liam?" I asked, confused. "Why are you not concerned about everything that's happening?"

He laughed, squeezing me tight. "Because. Selene is just here to make sure I'm doing my part, which I am. After tonight, my best friend will be immortal and I no longer have to spend every spare moment wondering if she's dead. And you're staying with me. You aren't going to leave and I don't have to mourn what would have been."

I supposed that did all sound good. I arched up to kiss him before breaking away.

"See you on stage," I breathed, and he blew me one more kiss.

For everything that was happening around us, the show went off reasonably flawlessly. Of course, in such a big production, with such a huge cast, there would always be hitches. And I was glad that Liam was on stage with me, most of the time, showing me how to react in the moment when things went wrong.

Twice, I forgot my line and he scooped up the words into his own, as if it were natural, so none of the plot got missed. One of the actresses who played a servant tripped over the table cloth while setting the table and Liam caught her with a beast-like growl and scolding that made the crowd roar with laughter. He even managed to put out a fire when a candle stick burned too low, snuffing it so fast that I didn't even notice anything had happened.

But what had me awed most of all was his talent. Liam was as spectacular as he had ever been in Hollywood, every line coming out smooth and clean. I had not thought of him as that Hollywood Superstar in a long time, but tonight, I felt like I should worship the ground he walked on. He was marvelous and brilliant, and I felt sad that the world he so loved had been ripped away from him one night.

Liam deserved every ounce of fame he had earned, and every chance he got. But instead, he was here, with me as his co-star. And as lucky as that made me, I hated Selene every second for doing this to him.

The show went by so fast that I barely noticed when we came to the end.

The final scene was the biggest of the show, of course. Everyone was gathering in the wings and trickling on stage to see the union of Beauty and her Prince. I was on top of the world. I had seen my father in the front row and he seemed entranced by the whole show, sitting unmoving with a bouquet of roses in his lap. And even though this first show was over, we still had three more weeks to play and I could rest in Liam's arms on and off stage.

I almost didn't see her in the wings as we went to take our first bows. Flowers and teddy bears were being thrown up on the stage, flying by us. The other actors were giggling and ducking. The children who were in the audience had smiles lighting up their faces and making their eyes twinkle. For two hours, they had forgotten their own troubles and illnesses, and had lived in the world of magic that we had created. This was the reason I wanted to act for the rest of my life.

She must have been watching the whole time, because she would have had to time her arrival perfectly. Everyone after the final curtain call was to exit stage right and head to the lobby immediately, so that the audience would be greeted by what appeared to be the continuation of the ball when they exited the theater. I happened to turn my head at the right moment, and I saw the cloud of dark and red hair standing in the wings. And somehow, I knew Porsche standing peacefully in the wings with Selene wasn't likely.

"Liam," I breathed, trying not to attract attention as we took a second bow. He turned to me, a wide grin on his face.

"Uh huh?"

I bobbed my head subtly towards the wings. He raised an eyebrow and leaned back, and I saw his eyes widen. Turning his head toward the stagehand on the left, he indicated the curtain should fall after our third bow. I still heard endless amounts of applause, and the cast seemed disappointed to not be receiving it, but Liam took charge, immediately.

"All of you, to the lobby now. Go," he boomed, and they went, without a word. Most of them were grinning and slapping each other on the back. "You should go too, Amy," he said, and I shook my head, meeting his eyes. There was no way I was leaving him now, not when I had just gotten him back.

"No. This is no longer just your fight. I'm involved too, whether you like it or not."

"Fine." He narrowed his eyes, taking my hand. "But, at the first sign of trouble, you bolt. Run. You understand me?"

"Yes." I nodded and took his hand. If he was to face Selene, then I was going to be standing by his side.

When we were finally alone on the stage, Liam turned casually towards the wings, as if we were just wandering in the wrong direction.

As we got closer, I tensed up. Selene was standing behind Porsche, who looked rigid and uncomfortable, her jaw set. Her eyes were wide and she was trying to warn us off, I could see it. But Liam, my brave Liam, was having none of it.

"Ah, my beautiful Liam. What a performance." Selene's French accent was thick, but it only added to her beauty. She truly was the most beautiful woman I had ever seen in my life. But the evil that lay behind her eyes brought the reality home for me. This was a woman to be feared, to be hated.

"Porsche, are you alright?" Liam asked, ignoring Selene. Porsche shrugged, although I could see she was petrified.

"Sure," she managed. Liam took a step closer and Selene growled at him.

"Don't move, boy."

"What is it I can do for you?" Liam asked her, calmly, as if this were a normal conversation. "You came to check on me, Selene, same as last year. And so here I am. Operating the school, flying under the radar, acting human and sucking blood bags. So what is it you want? Let go of Porsche before I rip you limb from limb," he said it mildly, as if they were talking about the weather. But I could see his eyes darken, and I knew he meant it.

"But you aren't," Selene replied, and her eyes darted to me. "You aren't exactly keeping what you are a secret, are you, Liam?"

"Amy, get behind me," he growled, not giving me a choice in the matter. His arm pulled me back, but I fought to face Selene.

"Are you talking about me?" I asked, with more courage in my voice than I ever had in my life. "Yes, Liam told me what he was. But I would never ever tell anyone. I didn't even want to believe it myself. "

"Ah, little one, your integrity does not factor into the vampire code. Liam's job was to keep everything quiet, and yet I see two humans here who know what we are," she replied, and Liam smirked.

"Except you seem to be breathing right now, Selene, so may I remind you that I could snap your neck like a twig in one move. Let go of Porsche, now." I could see he meant it too, his fist clenching at his side. Never in my whole life had I ever wanted anyone to die, until tonight. Anger burned up inside me until I was seeing red. I wanted nothing more than to see Selene running for her life, and then lifeless on the floor.

"Kill me, Liam, and you know what happens." Her voice was ominous, and my mind was spinning.

"But I'm dying too!" I blurted out, and everyone turned to me. "I mean...I will. Sooner than a normal person. Like Porsche, I'm also HIV positive. So even though I know Liam's secret...it's not like I'm going to know it for 100 years."

"Amy." Liam's face softened as he turned to me. "Don't talk like that."

"It's the truth."

Porsche whimpered and squirmed and we both turned back. Selene had her arm twisted behind her back and I could see she was hurting her. Liam met Porsche's eyes and raised an eyebrow. Very slowly, Porsche gave the tiniest nod.

I felt my stomach plummet. Here, it was going to happen here and now, and I was going to be witness to it. Porsche would accept the death sentence Liam gave her and transform into a vampire. My eyes were darting around the theater, trying to think of an exit plan to get Porsche and I out, when all of sudden, Selene laughed.

"Liam, such a pretty face, but you aren't very smart, are you? But then, I guess that's always been the case, failing to do your research. That's what you were famous for, wasn't it? Showing up on set having no idea what the movie was even about?"

"Selene..." Liam's grip on my arm tightened. "Let. Her. Go."

"Why?" she asked. "It's not going to make a difference."

She twisted, and Porsche doubled over. She gagged twice and then threw up, her legs trembling. My heart went out for her and I closed my eyes, leaning against Liam.

"Liam, make her better," I whispered. "Let it end for her, please."

Selene threw her head back and laughed, seemingly unaffected by Porsche's pain.

"I can grant that wish. Let me be exceptionally clear to you, Liam, because you and your little performer friends have always been stupid. This lovely beautiful ballerina here is a Shield, as you know. A Shield blocks all supernatural powers. All of them. And she is a very powerful Shield indeed, probably one of the most powerful I've ever seen. It's a shame, really." She jerked Porsche upward, an arm around her neck tightly. Liam tensed, ready to pounce.

"Yes," he said, confirming every fact. "But Porsche's existence is not to end."

"And how do you propose that, exactly?" Selene asked. "You can bind a Shield to you so that she will serve you, and your powers won't be as affected. In return, you can give her protection for her family, money, happiness in the bedroom, whatever it was she sought. But you cannot change the fact that her blood is supernaturally resistant. You cannot transform a Shield, Liam. They are doomed to be mortal, forever."

CHAPTER 24: LIAM

I felt the world rumble at Selene's statement. Porsche's glazed eyes looked up to meet mine in horror, her jaw unclenching to scream. It must have happened fast, but it felt like slow motion. I was already trying to calculate what to do when Selene's arm muscles tensed around Porsche's neck, and in less than a second, my beautiful ballerina was lying limp on the floor.

"NOOOO!" I howled, and was struck by a bolt of pain, as I felt my transformation rush into me. It nearly crippled me and I half fell, half stumbled toward her body, grabbing for her neck. Her head bobbed around like a ragdoll, her eyes lifeless and looking skyward.

I sunk my fast growing fangs into her trachea, the spot of transformation. If you wanted to drink blood, you drank from the side of the neck and could leave the body half drained without fear. But if you wanted to sire someone, you bit the front, on either side of the trachea.

Porsche's blood was rancid and I nearly gagged. My transformation was rushing through my body, trying to make up for lost time. It was disorientating and painful as my heart suddenly stopped and I found I couldn't breathe.

But what was the most painful of all was that her body remained limp, despite the fact that my venom should have been seeping into her veins. She had been dead less than a minute, which was still well in the clear to transform. As long as the body was still warm, you had time.

But Porsche, my savior, my best friend, stayed dead.

I bit her again and again, nearly gouging out her broken throat.

"C'mon, baby," I said, giving her a little shake. "C'mon. Wake up. Wake up. You're stronger than this. There's no more pain on this side, no more disease. I promised you immortality, Porsche, and it's yours to have, you just have to take it. COME ON!"

Her body flopped around, her red hair flying across her face. She was so thin, and so clearly so sick, it must have been torture for her to last as long as she did. She had waited it out, given me that, and now, I had nothing to give her.

"Porsche," my voice came out broken, and I felt Amy kneel down next to me, taking my hand.

"Liam. Liam." She tried to pull me back. "She's gone, Liam."

"No!" I ripped away from Amy, biting into the ravaged throat once again. But it was no use, as I knew it wouldn't be. Her body was lifeless and she wasn't coming back.

I sank back onto my heels, my sobs coming in gasps. I didn't realize I could feel this way, fully transformed. I had never cried as a vampire, and it was worse than being human. Everything felt more intense, more unmanageable. I felt like that pain would never stop, never let up. It was only Amy's arms around me, warm and beating with life, that let me even think straight.

Amy was crying too, her face buried in my neck, but she was silent about it—the cry of one who had accepted fate.

And I guess she had to; this beautiful girl whom I loved more than anything. Amy had lost her mother and long since accepted that her own death would come sooner than others. She was in touch with both life and death; something I, in my three years as a vampire, had never been able to accept. There was a wisdom about her that was far superior to her years. Her eyes were full of understanding that I could never hope to gain.

"There's another life, you know," Amy said, through her tears. "It's not just...human or vampire. There's a whole other existence out there, a whole other place where there's happiness and no pain. And that's where she is now, Liam."

"This is my fault," I managed, unable to look at the body that lay just beyond us.

"It's not," Amy said, sitting up to meet my eyes. Her eyes were clear, despite the tears. "This is *not* your fault. You did not make the choice to do this, Liam. Your choice was to save her, and hers was to save you. It was Selene who interfered with all that, and the death is on her hands." She was inches from my face, and this time, there was no recoiling or flinching at my appearance. I knew I must be in full vampire mode, but Amy didn't seem to care. She was gazing upon me as if I was fully human.

"Selene." I looked up, suddenly, remembering.

"She ran," Amy said. "Transformed as well. As soon as Porsche..." She reached up to wipe tears from her face.

"She'll be back," I said, shakily. "She always is. And she'll pay, for what she did. For taking more than one life that was not hers to take. "

I wanted to get up, run, anywhere, do something. But I knew it was no use. Selene would be long gone by now. She was centuries old, and I had no hope of finding her if she did not want to be found. The smartest thing to do was wait, wait until she came back, which I knew she would.

I crawled forward a few paces. Even in death, Porsche was beautiful. I closed her eyes and it had the effect that she was sleeping. As if my redheaded beauty would wake at any moment. But she would not; not from her eternal slumber.

215

The grief struck me hard, and had it not been for Amy's steadying grip, I would have joined her.

"I love you." I turned to Amy, whose eyes widened in shock. It wasn't the best moment, but I had to say it. "I love you, and I have pretty much since the first day I met you. And I don't think I can live without you, Amy, so please say you're not going anywhere."

"I already told you I'm not," she said, softly. "I'm not. Ever. I love you too, Liam. I'm sorry I ran from you. I shouldn't have."

"No." I shook my head. "You had every right to. This love, Amy, this love is not easy. It's probably going to be the hardest thing in the world. And it's dangerous. Selene knows that you know now, and she's right, you shouldn't. But I promise I will do everything in my power to protect you. Because I don't think I can do this alone, my love. I can't be alone any longer."

"You never were." She placed a hand over mine. We sat in silence for a long moment, each lost in our own thoughts. Finally, she spoke, "Should I call 9-1-1? I mean...I know there's nothing...but..."

"Yes." I nodded, running a hand over my face. "One of her pet peeves was theater shows getting delayed. She'd probably kill me if she knew we were sitting here right now, instead of going to accept our audience. They'll be waiting for us."

"We can't just...leave her here," Amy said.

"We can." I took one last look at her before standing up. "Porsche's part in this tale is done, although I will never forget her. Call 9-1-1, Amy, and tell them we found her dead. I will not have her name buried under a murder investigation. "

216

"They'll know." Amy wiped her eyes. "They'll know something is wrong. Look at her throat."

"They'll know," I agreed. "But the world doesn't have to. Porsche De Ritter will remain a beautiful ballerina who slipped away."

Amy nodded, already dialing the number on her cell phone. I closed my eyes, trying to regain control of all my limbs. None of this seemed real. The underlying feeling was anger. I wanted to go mad, to find Selene and rip her apart and make sure she suffered in her last moments as Porsche did. Had Amy not been in my life, I would have wanted to go on a rampage—hunt down the French vampire and her kind until nothing remained. And then likely, I would have thrown myself off a bridge into a watery grave.

But Amy made all the difference. She stood, her shoulders tensed with courage as she spoke to the 9-1-1 operator, and she looked up at me, offering me the tiniest smile. Without her, I would be nothing more than a monster. But with her in my life, her heart beating strong and fierce, I had a chance to live again.

"It's done," she said, hanging up the phone. "They'll be here soon."

"Can you make me look presentable?" I asked her, angling my head so there was light on it. "The world should know that she's gone. Let's make tonight for her."

"I uh…I can try," she replied, eyeing my makeup.

"Wait." I turned back to Porsche, taking a deep breath to steel myself. Leaning down, I planted a kiss on her cheek, which was now cold. "Dance in heaven, princess," I whispered, trying not to let the tears fall again. "Thank you, for everything. I'll be alright. Amy will help me be alright. No more pain now."

217

I closed my eyes, trying to accept the reality that lay before me. After a moment, I rose, taking Amy's hand to steady myself.

"Let's go give her a final curtain call," I said, and Amy nodded.

Her makeup job wasn't perfect, but between the two of us, we managed to make me look human. I felt sick inside, and craved no blood, which I supposed could only help me. Any lingering vampire appearance could be explained away by the fact that my Beast makeup hadn't been properly removed.

On shaking legs, and with Amy's help, we climbed the staircase in the lobby, taking our place on the balcony. As soon as we appeared, the audience waiting below burst into applause. Camera flashes went off and cheers went up. I closed my eyes, taking Amy's hand. She squeezed it tight, nodding to me with encouragement.

"Thank you," I spoke into the microphone that had been carefully placed. "But your applause is not just for me tonight, but for the hundreds of people who helped make this production happen. I could not have done it alone. None of us want to do anything alone." I swallowed, careful not to let my eyes shine with tears. Amy squeezed my hand again and I waited until the crowd was completely silent. "Without Amy...my Beauty, I could not have felt what the Beast felt on stage. Amy, from our first meeting, had a very special place in my heart, and she will continue to do so as we continue both our professional...and personal relationship next year."

The crowd gasped, and Amy gasped as well. I could only offer her a smile though. I was sick of hiding from the whole world; hiding everything and keeping everything a secret. I loved her, and I wanted everyone to know that. To reinforce what I said, I leaned in, kissing her gently on the lips.

"I do love you," I told her, and she nodded, stunned. "And there's no use hiding it anymore."

"I love you too," she whispered, delivering me another kiss while the crowd went wild. Finally, we broke apart and I turned back to the microphone, my job not yet done. Loving Amy was the easy part. Telling them what I had to tell them next was hard.

"I also..." I swallowed hard. "I also couldn't have done this play without a very good friend of mine. Porsche De Ritter..." I almost choked on saying her name, but managed to continue. "Porsche was my first scholarship winner, although her time here was short..."

Amy choked at this, turning away slightly.

"She danced for the Russian National Ballet for 3 years as their Prima Donna, and she had quite a future ahead of her. She always found time to help out here, however, the place that gave her the start she needed...As many of you know, Porsche also suffered from AIDS, and it became harder to work as she got sicker. However she never faltered on her commitments and her dedication to helping me with this show..." I trailed off, not knowing where to go from here. I scanned the crowd, and saw students, teachers and the media holding their breath. "It is with great sadness that I announce Porsche's passing, early this evening. True to form, she made sure Beauty and the Beast went on without a hitch." I raised a glass someone handed me and the crowd did the same, in stunned silence. "So to Porsche. And to Amy." I put an arm around her. "And to unconventional love."

It was as I knocked back the champagne that I spotted her in the crowd. She had on sunglasses and her mouth was closed, and so it was enough to hide what she really was. But Selene stood there, in the center of everyone, looking up at me with a sneer.

"Forever," she mouthed at me, making time stand still for just that moment. And then Amy hugged me, and Selene was gone, as if she just melted away.

If my heart was beating it would have been beating swiftly at that moment. As Amy hugged me, and the crowd drank to my toast, and I focused on the spot where Selene was. I realized I needed to end this, once and for all. For Porsche, and for Amy.

CHAPTER 25 - AMY

For three weeks, life almost felt normal again. A great sadness had come over the school, but it pushed us to be better at our work, at the show, at everything. It reminded us that life was short, and we should take every opportunity we could get.

And so we did. My friends and I began to go out more and seeing the city as never before. We had long talks at the cafeteria tables about our hopes and dreams and how we wanted to make them a reality. While Charisma was excellent at acting, she revealed what she really wanted to do was be a director. Another girl piped up with her dreams of a screenplay, and soon, we had a full movie plotted out to be shot and filmed when I returned from my Gatsby tour.

We talked about love, and loss. I discovered more than one girl had lost a parent, and some had no memories of anything but single parent life. I showed them the very few surviving photographs of my mom that I had, and we shared in the grief.

We talked about drugs, about disease and death. It was no secret that Porsche contracted AIDS from a dirty needle and because of her lifestyle choice that she should have done without. For the first time, the hard partiers in the group began to realize that there was more to life than the dark of the night.

And of course, we talked about Liam. Although I didn't want to share too much, everyone wanted to know the details of our love affair. I shared what I could, the difficulty of being together despite the age and status difference. Charisma told me she had once dated a man twenty years older than her, which of course, caused the others to gasp. The attention turned away from me, and as I listened, I realized how lucky I was, despite all of this tragedy. If anyone had told me what my life would be like a year ago, I would have laughed in their face. But now, I was happy. Truly happy.

221

My father, of course, took that as an opportunity to sit down and grill Liam within an inch of his life. Quite the opposite of their meeting in the fall, when it was Liam lording over both of us; I almost laughed as I watched him sit across from my father at lunch and squirm uncomfortably at questions about his intentions and his integrity.

"No, sir, of course, I won't keep her up late. I don't like being up late. In fact, you'll never see me after sunset," Liam swore, looking my father straight in the eye across our family dinner table. "Amy's future success and happiness is always my main concern."

"And no sleepovers," my father said, returning the look. Liam seemed to shrink in his chair, and nodded, blushing furiously. "Good. Looks like we'll get along then, Headmaster."

"Yes," Liam replied, although he wouldn't look away from his food. I smiled, cutting into mine. The fact that Liam had never had a serious relationship before didn't really throw me off. Neither had I, although our upbringings had been very different. At first, I had been terrified of what my father might say when he found out. But now, I saw that he just had my safety in mind, and wanted to make sure Liam made me happy. Which, I assured him, he did.

Since Liam's announcement, it seemed like the whole world knew within a matter of hours. He had assured the press that we fell in love after my acceptance to the school not before. And although those rumors still swelled, it didn't matter. Those close to us knew the truth.

My graduation papers had been scrapped, and I would return for another year after Gatsby went on tour this summer. I had not gotten the TV audition, no surprise there, but Liam had stepped in to offer his assistance and get me a proper talent agent. With Liam's guidance, I began to learn the ins and outs of the industry beyond what the school taught me. How to spot a scam;

how to know when it's ok to laugh in an audition and when you have to stay stoic. How to get your name and face noticed without being in the way.

Having passed all of my courses, my final year would be more of an independent study, in which I was expected to put a production of my own, overseeing all aspects. Ideas were already swirling in my head as I thought of what I would do; everything from serious dramas to full Broadway productions. I was amazed at how much work went into a production, and I realized whatever I put on would truly have to make me happy all year because it was going to take up all of my time.

But this was not the time to think about it. Having closed Beauty and the Beast last night, we were to head to the theater after lunch for a different kind of show. Porsche's funeral.

The Russian National Ballet had, in cooperation with Liam, flown in to put on one final show; a final goodbye to their young Prima Donna. I was trying not to think about it, sitting in the theater seats where she had sat only a few weeks ago surrounded by people who had known and loved her. Porsche's family, having never actually appeared in person, had requested that the results of her autopsy be kept a secret, much to our relief. To the world, the ballerina passed away from an AIDS related infection that took her life suddenly, but not unexpectedly. Already, I knew the Russian National had replaced her and life would move on.

But as lunch ended and we separated to get changed, it was getting harder and harder.

"How is everything?" Sarah asked, as I put her on speakerphone an hour later, rummaging around my room for my black outfit.

"It's...ok," I replied, pulling off my clothes to put the dress over my head. "I mean, as ok as can be expected. Liam's sad, of course, and I miss her...but we're ok. He took me out for pizza yesterday before the show and we had a good time. Sometimes..." I took a deep breath, looking at myself in the mirror. "Sometimes I think my heart will burst from loving him so much. This is like, Hollywood Movie type love. I thought it was fake."

"It is a Hollywood Romance." Sarah sighed happily on the other side of the phone. "And trust me, I know all about it because even here, the tabloid magazines tell me your every move. How was your pepperoni pizza with olives, by the way?"

"Shut up." I laughed, a rare occurrence in the past few weeks, as I swept my hair up into a bun. "Did you submit your application yet for the school? Deadlines for the graduate program are only a few days away."

Liam had decided to branch out and offer a graduate program next year that would be housed in a small building just off campus. He wanted no more than 10 students to try it out, and I, of course, had recommended Sarah. She didn't know yet, but I was pretty sure all I had to do was say the word and Liam would let her in.

"I'm just finishing it up," she replied. "I'm so excited. We could spend all next year together!"

"Well, regardless, I'll see you in a few weeks," I said, putting a final pin in my hair.

"Yes, I can't wait to see you in Gatsby, chorus member number 5," she teased me, and I rolled my eyes.

"I should go, Sarah. It's almost time."

"Yeah," her voice dropped a note. "I wish I could be there for you, Amy."

"Soon enough." I smiled sadly as I went to the phone. "Soon enough. I'll talk to you later."

"Bye," she said, and hung up, leaving me alone in the silence of the room.

A knock came at the door, and I opened it. Liam stood there, head to toe in black as well.

"Hey," I said. "You ready?"

"As ready as I'll ever be," he replied. "Amy, there's a lot of paparazzi outside, all right? I just wanted to warn you."

"They can't even give us a moment's peace, for a funeral?" I asked, as I locked my door and we headed toward the theater. Liam sighed.

"This is...the life I chose. But it doesn't have to be yours."

"Don't be silly," I said, taking his arm. "It is, and there's no way out of it."

Had we not had reserved seats in the theater, we never would have gotten in. Every seat and aisle was packed with people who knew Porsche and who would miss her terribly.

Taking Liam's hand at the start of the service, I bit my lip, resolving not to cry. I wanted to be strong for him. However, when the Corps de Ballet came out onto the stage and performed a short piece behind a holographic video of my friend, I couldn't stop the tears.

Liam, however, was looking straight ahead, his eyes almost unseeing as he watched. He had no tears, although his eyes were dark and his jaw was set. He held my hand throughout the entire service, and he spoke a eulogy that would break even the hardest of hearts. But it seemed he had resolved to let no one see what he was feeling.

Porsche was buried in a cemetery in the center of the city "where everyone will see her all the time" Liam had said, with a half-smile.

The service at the cemetery was smaller, and more private. I recognized almost everyone surrounding the grave from the funeral, except for a group off to the side. Most of them with flaming red hair as well, they kept to themselves, almost as if they were lurkers. They also didn't cry, but looked on with stony faces, as the dirt covered her grave.

"Liam," I said when they had finally disturbed me to the point where I had to say something. He looked up then, as if recovering from a coma.

"Huh?"

"There. Them. Who are they?" I nodded in their direction and he followed my eye line. Finally, for the first time in hours, I saw him react.

"Hm, I was expecting they'd be here," he said, watching. One of them looked up and met his eyes before turning and whispering to the group. "They're Shields: the Camerons, the McIntoshes and the De Ritters. I don't think any of them are the *official* Shields for their bloodlines, the ones with the most power, but they all carry it. They probably know who the next one is already."

"And they want to talk to you," I said, watching as the same one tried to catch Liam's eye.

226

He sighed, letting go of my hand. His beautiful eyes met mine. They glistened with deep sorrow and a strange resolve that unnerved me. "I want you to stay here, Amy."

"Sure," I replied, although I was thoroughly confused. He gave me a quick kiss on the cheek and then let go of my hand, heading off.

The Shields surrounded him immediately. I could see from his body posture he was in no danger, but curiosity was burning through me. What was it that they wanted? And what was Liam planning?

EPILOGUE - LIAM

I approached the Shields cautiously. They were giving me looks that should have burned holes through my skin and I had to force myself to smile as I approached. I held out my hand. Not to my great surprise, none of them took it.

"I'm Liam," I said. "It's good of you to come. I knew Porsche very well and I'm very sorry for your loss."

"Her body was defiled," one of them growled at me. It took every ounce of will I had to stand my ground. "Her throat was gouged out."

I looked around to make sure no one was listening and then lowered my voice. "Yes, and I'm sorry for that. In return for her service, Porsche wanted immortality, a life with no pain. I realize this is against everything you stand for...but Porsche was a friend, my best friend, and it was her choice. I didn't...I didn't know that it was an impossible promise, and neither did she. She died a hero, saving my life and the life of my...Amy." I wasn't sure what to say.

There was a long silence, and then at last one of them—a man in his fifties—stepped forward with his hand extended. "I am Thomas De Ritter," he said. "Porsche was my daughter."

"I'm so sorry for your loss, sir," I said, with as much respect as I could. Porsche had rarely spoken of her parents, having left home at a young age to pursue a career in dance that they didn't believe in. On a few drunken nights she had told me stories of them breaking her dreams and not believing in her talent; stories I could share. My own parents were across the ocean, still shaking their heads that their son played make-believe for a living. I could only imagine their reaction if I explained to them I was also a vampire.

"We had our differences, but you made her dream come true. And I believe she was happy in the last years of her life, and for that I thank you."

"She was very happy," I said, in memory. "Dancing was all she ever wanted to do."

"Well, then, I thank you for helping her," he replied, and there was another pause, as I tried to gather the courage for what I wanted to say next.

"I was wondering, sir... if you wanted to help me. Not as payback, by any means, but as assistance to living by your code."

This attracted the attention of the whole group, who turned to me. I took a deep breath. I felt incredibly human and I had no doubt that part of that came from being with them. My nerves made me feel like it was my first stage show.

"How?" he asked. His eyes that looked so much like Porsche's were fixed on me.

"Well, sir, what if I asked for your assistance in getting rid of two vampires?"

"Who?" Thomas shot back, clearly interested, but not dropping his guard any further. I bit my lip and looked around once more to check that Amy was still too far away to hear what I was about to say:

"My sire, Selene. And consequently, myself."

Want to read the next part of Amy and Liam's story?

Just visit: www.forrestbooks.com, enter your email address and I promise you'll be the first to know when the next book is released.

Thank you for reading!

Bella x

You might also want to check out my other novels:

A Shade Of Vampire (#1 Christmas Best seller in Vampire Romance, Paranormal & Fantasy.)

A Shade Of Blood

Visit: **www.bellaforrest.net** for details.

About The Author

I guess my life as a writer started when I was five; I'd sit under the kitchen table with my box of multi-colored wax crayons (I miss those) and create picture books. Creative writing was always my favorite subject and I used any free time I had to sit down with a notepad.

Not much has changed, except that now I have developed vampirish habits: my writing "day" typically starts at 1am.

I'm an avid reader, a big fan of cookie ice cream and I'm often travelling.

Don't forget to come say hello on Twitter and Facebook! I'd love to meet you personally:

www.facebook.com/AShadeOfVampire

www.twitter.com/AShadeOfVampire